1.14

by Åke Edwardson
Translated by Per Carlsson

SKYSCAPE

SKYSCAPE

Amazon Children's Publishing
P.O. Box 400818
Las Vegas, NV 89140
www.amazon.com/amazonchildrenspublishing

Library of Congress Cataloging-in-Publication Data available upon request.

9781477816547 (hardcover)
1477816542 (hardcover)
9781477866542 (eBook)
B00BHIFQ76 (eBook)

Book design by Sammy Yuen

Printed in the United States of America (R)
First edition
10 9 8 7 6 5 4 3 2 1

1

I wish this was a secret story. Sometimes I wish there wasn't even a story to tell. Maybe it would have been better for everyone. But then I think the opposite. The best thing that could have happened did happen.

It's late evening now. Darkness is setting in, and the whole camp lies still. There's a ceiling lamp giving off a blue glow that doesn't quite reach the ground. I'm sitting on the dirt floor. The light way up there in the sky is the moon.

I've been sitting here for a long time, and lying next to me is my long sword, my *katana*. It almost looks like a shadow on the floor in this light. My short sword, my *wakizashi*, is in my belt. I can feel its handle when I move, but I'm not going to move. I'm not going to do anything, not right now. I have a story to tell.

There's still some light outside because it's summer. The end of what has been my last summer. I hope to be able to explain that eventually if I can. But I'm not sure you can explain anything. Things happen, sometimes because they have to, sometimes even though they don't have to. And the most terrible things are the ones that are the most difficult to explain.

There are almost no walls left around me where I'm sitting. I can hear sounds in the night. A bird screeches out over the lake. I've heard it before—I think it's the same one. It seems to be as sleepless as I am. It's the only bird that screeches as it flies around in the sky above the lake. Maybe it's flying in its sleep. Maybe it screeches in its sleep and drives the other seabirds crazy. In the morning the grebes are so tired they almost drown when they dive beneath the surface for fish.

This story is about the lake and the forest.

I turned twelve last spring. Mama and Papa christened me Tommy, but my name is Kenny and nothing else. That's the name I took when I baptized myself last summer. I stood in a stream and poured water onto the blade of my sword until the water turned to blood. Then I drew it across my forehead and became Kenny. The name comes from the Japanese word for sword: *ken*.

I'm a *samurai*. In Japan you're born a *samurai*, and when you're five years old you're given your *samurai* garb and a sword. I wasn't so lucky.

The sleepless bird lets out another screech in the darkness. It's not as clear as before. I feel a little tired, but this is going to be a long night.

2

I get so angry sometimes, all of a sudden, and then I might call someone I don't even know a bloody bastard! I can tell you I've cursed a lot in my life. I don't really know why. Mama doesn't swear. She's told me not to a million times but it doesn't help.

I always used to get into fights at home in the front yard, just like that, without even thinking about it.

But I've stopped that now. A samurai is always calm. I may not be a full-fledged samurai yet—someone who's always as calm as a rock—but it's just a question of practice. If I swear sometimes, it's because my soul hasn't yet evolved into the perfect state: *satori*. That's when the soul and the sword become one. The sword is no longer a weapon but something you need in order to feel at peace. But then you also have to become a master swordsman.

———+———

I tried to sneak off after breakfast every morning to practice not getting angry. It wasn't easy. There were forty prisoners at the camp. It started in the morning when everyone had to go out to the toilets and then make their beds and put away their stuff. There were ten of us boys living in my dormitory. Across from us was another dormitory with ten boys, and below us were two girls' dorms. Sometimes you could hear something from down there. Somebody crying, probably for their mother.

One night I heard a howl through the floor. I thought about it the next day, but I never found out what it was. You hardly ever heard any laughter from the girls' dorms. You would have heard it if there had been any. Laughter carried through anything. But at this camp we weren't meant to laugh. If anyone did laugh they were just faking it. It hurt your throat.

There was no way you could practice staying calm during breakfast either, not with forty spoons clattering against forty plates. There was sort of an echo, so it sounded like eighty spoons clattering away until the oatmeal was finished, and the quicker it was finished the better because it tasted like chicken poop.

We washed ourselves in the lake twice a day. We could

do that before breakfast if we wanted to. That was the one thing the counselors didn't care about. I guess they were just waking up then. They were always up late at night.

As for me, I always took my time washing myself because the samurai were careful about keeping themselves clean. But some were sloppy about washing themselves. Sausage, for example, from my dorm. But not even Sausage escaped when everyone had to get washed with hot water and soap in the bathtubs. It happened once in the middle of the summer in the evening before the mothers and fathers were supposed to come visit. I guess the idea was for everyone to smell good when it was visiting time. If they only knew what it smelled like otherwise.

The evening before visiting day, we received fresh sheets that also smelled good—almost like the forest out there during the day. The sheets were a little harder, too, and it was more difficult to make the beds with them the first morning. You had to make an effort if you wanted to win the bed-making contest.

Once I said to one of the counselors that I wanted to take a bath more than once a summer. She just looked at me. She didn't get it. I think it was last summer or the summer before that. Sometimes all the summers flow together like different streams flowing into the spring when the water's high.

I've been at the camp more summers than anyone. Only

Matron has been here more summers than me, but that's not so strange considering she's the overseer and was already here back when I was still in Mama's belly.

Mama was here a few weeks ago on the big Visiting Day. As usual, she had walked from the turnoff by the main road where the bus stopped. She had trudged two miles through the woods, and as always, she smelled of sweat when she got here.

She had brought a bag of Twist chocolates with her that the counselors stole. Unless it was Matron herself who took it.

First I got to hold it, but then I had to hand it over to the counselors. That was how things were done here. The candy would then be distributed among all the kids, if you were lucky. When I didn't get a piece of chocolate that night or the next, I realized they had taken the bag.

On visiting day, Mama carried the bag of Twist through the forest. Once she had caught her breath after her trek, she sat down on one of the chairs outside the woodshed. She wiped her face with this old handkerchief that was so sheer you could see right through it. It was like a window. I saw Mama's face on the other side of it. I knew it was her, of course, but there was still something different about her. Like she wasn't quite the same this time. Like the bag of Twist meant something. She had never brought along anything that special before.

She stuffed the handkerchief into her handbag, which was round like a soccer ball.

"Your hair's getting long, Tommy," Mama said.

I didn't answer. Mama pushed her own hair back, which was brown and curly and sort of uneven across her forehead. Maybe she had cut it herself. She had looked exactly the same for as long as I could remember.

"Your hair has almost gone white from the sun," she said.

She looked out across the lake, which was gleaming so brightly that it hurt your eyes. It was white from the sun, and it seemed like I had turned the same color. She looked at me again.

"It really is unusually hot this summer."

I still said nothing.

"Tommy?"

"You know what my name is," I said.

"Tommy," she said again, but this time it wasn't a question anymore. She looked out at the lake again, as though Tommy were out there somewhere. But all she could see was a boat far in the distance—a canoe perhaps. It was just like a piece of black construction paper against all that white.

"How are things in town?" I asked. I had to change the

focus because it hurt my eyes to keep looking at the lake like I was looking for that Tommy kid too.

I wanted her to look at me again.

"Same as ever," she said and turned her head, "only warmer." She picked up her handkerchief and mopped her brow. "Somehow, it seems to get hotter in town than in the countryside in the summer."

"Don't ask me," I said.

"You do like being out here, don't you, Tommy?"

I didn't answer.

"Ke-Kenny." I saw that she had to make an effort to say my real name. "You do like it out here, don't you?"

"I don't have anything to compare it to," I said.

"You can go swimming and diving every day," she said. She made it sound like I was a fish or something.

"There's a swimming pool in town," I said.

"It's always full there. You should see it."

"Yeah, right."

She looked around.

"Of course, this is your last summer here."

I didn't answer.

"Then you'll have to get used to summers in the city."

"I guess you'll find some other place to send me off to."

"That's not fair, Tommy."

"Who's Tommy?" I asked.

"Kenny then." It sounded like a sigh when she said it.

She knew nothing about fairness, but I didn't want to say that to her. She wouldn't understand.

"If Papa were around I wouldn't have been stuck in this penitentiary," I said.

She probably thought that wasn't fair either, but she didn't say anything. Then I felt strange. Maybe I had said more than I ought to. And much more than a samurai would have said. It wasn't her fault that Papa wasn't home. It wasn't anyone's fault. He was just gone all of a sudden. That was three years ago. He'd said goodbye, and then he'd gone out and had never come back.

At the funeral, his hair was long and it was bleached white by the sun. I went up and said goodbye to him. Mama bawled like a cow in the church. Her wails echoed against all the walls. I wanted her to be quiet. I don't know why, but I wanted the church to be completely silent right then. Deathly silent.

After that, they sent my mother off to some rest home. They wouldn't let me live by myself at home so I had to stay with Grandma, but she could barely walk so that wasn't much of a rest home for me.

As I was standing there next to my dad lying in his casket, I started to think about death, which wasn't so strange, of course. And when I learned more about how it is to be a samurai, I came to understand what death is. It's nothing. You should expect to die every day. That way you're prepared for it, and when that day comes you'll be calm. It's nothing to fear.

Every morning the samurai looks for a peaceful place to clear his head of all the things that aren't peaceful thoughts. Then he tries to imagine himself at the exact moment, the very second, that he's pierced by an arrow or a rifle bullet or a lance or a sword. Thrown into a fire. Struck by lightning. Crushed in an earthquake. Hurled from a cliff. Overcome by disease. Or run over by a train.

Maybe all of them at once.

The samurai say: "Die each day in your mind. Then you will not fear death. Think of death every morning and every night."

"Kenny?" I heard Mama's voice. It sounded far away, as if she were sitting in another world.

"What?" I said after a while.

"You went so quiet."

"Wasn't I the last one who spoke?"

"You looked like you were thinking about something," she said.

"It'd be strange if I weren't thinking about something, wouldn't it? Aren't you always thinking about something?"

"What were you thinking about then?" she asked with a smile.

"Nothing," I answered.

I didn't tell Mama about what happened to my bag of Twist. I wanted to clear that up myself.

The sun was still up when Mama left, but it was evening. We were alone again, all forty of us. A few of the girls cried, but they did it silently. One of them was sitting by herself on the thick branch that reached out over the cove where we washed ourselves every morning and evening.

I don't know why I went there. Maybe I had seen something ripple on the surface of the water. A big pike. I don't think anyone saw me as I walked across the grass.

A couple of the smaller kids were spinning slowly on the merry-go-round without yelling or talking. Everyone seemed to be thinking about their mothers and fathers.

The girl sitting on the branch was Kerstin. I didn't know her but I knew the name of pretty much everyone here.

Kerstin wiped her eyes. She had long hair that was light and almost yellow in the sun. It hung down into her face a little.

"Hi," I said.

She nodded and brushed the hair away from her forehead.

I turned around to see if anyone could see us, but the courtyard was almost deserted. The two little kids on the merry-go-round had disappeared.

"How's it going?" I asked.

"Okay." she answered. That was it. It was probably the first time I'd heard her say anything.

Just then, a fish thrashed its tail among the reeds on the other side of the creek. It sounded like the shot from a cannon.

"That was probably Old Pike," I said.

"You think so?"

"Do you fish?" I asked.

"I don't have a pole," she said.

"You can whittle one. I've got a good knife."

I meant my hunting knife, not my short sword, my *wakizashi*.

"You need a line and hook, don't you?" she asked.

"I've got those. And floats too."

"Guess you've got everything then," she said as she jumped down from the branch.

"I'm saving up for a casting rod," I said. "I don't have one of those. And no reel either. I'm planning on buying an Ambassador Gold."

"Sounds expensive."

"It's the best."

Kerstin nodded. I think she understood. She was standing

next to me now just a few feet away. She was about the same age as me but a little taller. She looked strong. Maybe she would make a good girl samurai. Maybe she'd have a high rank.

The wife of a samurai was put in command of the regular soldiers when the samurai were away. Some samurai wives were good at fighting and self-defense. Once in the1500s, a samurai's wife climbed up onto the roof of her castle to spy on the enemy soldiers below. When she was done spying, she drew a map of their encampment with her lipstick.

Kerstin didn't wear any lipstick like Mama did, for example. I could always smell lipstick whenever Mama tried to hug me. It smelled awful.

"Want me to make you a fishing pole?" I don't know why I asked. I really hadn't planned on saying that.

"When?"

"Well . . . tomorrow?"

"Out in the forest?"

"Of course."

"I don't know," she said.

She looked as though she thought the forest was dangerous. She probably didn't know that the forest was a place where you could always be at peace. That's how I felt anyway.

But I was wrong.

"You don't have to come with me if you don't want to," I said.

"Do you have some special place in the forest?" she asked.

She pointed toward the woods beyond the creek as if I didn't know what a forest looked like.

There was no fence or barbed wire or anything around the camp. They were smarter than that. They knew we had nowhere to go—at least not for long. It was even scarier this way.

"We've got a castle," I said.

And with that, I had given it away. It was a secret we weren't allowed to tell anybody. Especially not a girl. The words just came out; I didn't have a chance to think about it.

"What sort of castle?"

I didn't answer.

"Are there others who have this castle?"

I nodded. I didn't want to say anything more.

"What sort of a castle is it?"

"I . . . can't tell you."

"Why not?"

"Because it's a secret."

"Then you shouldn't have told me, should you?"

She looked at me and smiled. This girl was smart. I had to watch myself.

"Sometimes I talk too much," I said.

"Can I see it?" she asked. "The castle?"

I didn't answer. I thought first. Yeah, this time I thought first. I had already told her she could come with me into the forest. And the forest *was* the castle in a way.

"Okay," I said.

I would live to regret that.

3

I t was evening again. We had just been down to the lake to wash ourselves. You came back dirtier than before you went down. When you dipped your hand into the water, it came out covered in a brown film that was almost like a second skin. It worked as protection against the sun. This summer the sun was intense. They said it was hotter than it had ever been.

When we were eating our supper there was a girl who threw up. Nice one! I think her name was Lena. The food was so disgusting that all forty of us should have thrown up every time we sat at the table, but nobody had dared do it before. Lena sat at the same long table as me, and suddenly she leaned forward and threw up. Stuff like that impressed me. Kerstin was sitting a few chairs away from Lena. I looked at Kerstin but she didn't look back. Instead she stood up and went over to Lena just as the counselors came running over. Otherwise it was deathly silent in the mess hall.

Then it started to smell. One of the counselors led Lena away so that the rest of us wouldn't throw up too. I looked down at my plate: two slimy prunes drowning in oatmeal. If I had thrown up into my plate it wouldn't have looked or tasted any different.

When we got up to the dormitory, Sausage made puking noises, but it wasn't funny anymore.

"Cut it out, Sausage."

"What?"

He looked like I'd just hit him. Like he was about to start blubbering just because I had said that.

"It was only funny down there," I said.

"Jeez," said Sausage and went over to his bed, sat down on it, and sulked. Then he looked up. "You didn't have to say that," he said.

"Yeah, yeah."

Then he perked up and asked, "Are we going to work on the camp tomorrow?" His head was round, and when he looked happy his face became even rounder. He was round all over and his mother only sent him clothes that were too tight for him. Maybe she hoped he would get thin enough that the clothes would fit. Her own clothes were always too big. When she came on visiting day it looked like a four-man tent had wandered in through the front gate.

"The castle," I said. "It's not a camp."

"Yeah, yeah, the castle."

"What else would we do?" It was Micke who said that. His bed was next to Sausage's. Micke was as skinny as a twig and as wiry as a juniper branch. When he and Sausage stood next to each other they looked like creatures from two different planets. Micke could never look plump. He was always unhappy, and I had never heard him laugh. It was like he didn't know how. He was directly below me in rank. When I was out on a mission, he was left in command. He was a good commander. He returned the command to me when I got back without saying much.

But once, earlier last summer, it seemed like he wasn't satisfied with going back to being number two again. It wasn't something I asked him about. It wasn't anything he said. It was just something I felt.

"What else would we do," Micke said again, "except work on the castle?"

Just then, I thought of Kerstin and what I had said to her. I still couldn't believe that I'd told her about the castle.

"Yeah, what else would we do?" said Sausage with a laugh.

"We have to widen the moat," said Micke.

"We have to dig the ditch from the creek first," said Lennart, who was sitting on his bed farther down.

"You can't widen the moat when it's full of water, can you?" asked Micke.

Lennart looked at him. Lennart was the same age as me and about as tall. We had the same color hair and sometimes the counselors got us mixed up. But I had ten times as many freckles as Lennart. And he never got sunburned, not even this summer.

He had been at the camp last summer, too, and we had become friends. He had no mother back home. Apparently she'd just left one day without leaving behind a letter or anything. That was tough on Lennart. He was the first one I had approached to be second in command, but he had said that he didn't want to be in charge of anyone but himself. He hadn't looked very happy when he said it. I thought a lot about that last summer. In charge of yourself? When did you ever get to decide anything for yourself? When you were a kid you didn't get to decide anything. At least not about yourself. It was the grown-ups who made all the decisions, even though they could barely look after themselves.

But at least we had the castle. And I had my troop. I was in charge of that—sometimes anyway. We had our own country.

"We're not going to dig all that way," said Lennart to Micke.

"But we have to dig a canal from the creek."

"But that'll take years," said Sausage. "It's miles and miles from the creek to the castle."

"We've got plenty of time," said Lennart.

"You sound like you want to stay here," said Micke.

"You got a better suggestion? Maybe you want me to come stay at your house in the fall?"

"I'm sure they'd be thrilled," said Micke. "Another mouth to feed."

"We can carry water from the creek and pour it into the moat," said Sausage.

We laughed at him.

We had a lot of work ahead of us. So far, we had mostly been working on the main tower. There was going to be a big hall where we could receive visitors. And guard towers and weapons stores. And the samurai leader's quarters—mine, that is. And then a hall for the warriors. But there was a lot left to build: the gatehouse, side towers, guard towers, inner courtyard, inner wall, outer courtyard, outer wall, and then the moat.

The troop consisted of Sausage, Micke, and Lennart, and then there were Janne, Sven-Åke and Mats too. Janne and Mats lived in our dormitory; Sven-Åke lived in the dorm opposite. He was also an old friend from last summer. All of them were good warriors except maybe for Sausage, but he was good in other ways. I didn't want anyone else in the troop. It might have been a good idea if there were more of us to help build the castle, but then we'd have to take care of the extra helpers afterward too. It wasn't a good idea to be too many. That could lead to mutiny. You can't be in command of too many warriors. Also, everybody has to have the chance to make their own decisions, and the bigger the troop, the more difficult that becomes.

I heard a bird screech out over the lake. It didn't sound like it usually did. It sounded like it was calling for help. I went over to the window. It was still light outside. I could hear laughter in the courtyard below. I hooked the window open and leaned out. A couple of the counselors were standing there. All the counselors were women. These two were all dressed up wearing skirts and stuff. They were laughing. The door to the building in the courtyard opened and I heard music coming from inside. Even though I hadn't seen it yet, I knew that one of the counselors had a record player. I had thought about taking it and keeping it at the castle, but there was no electricity out there so there was no point.

I heard them put on "Let's Twist Again," and that was about the only song I knew. It was good. I had heard it on the radio. It had nothing to do with bags of Twist. Then, thinking about that, I got the idea that I'd sneak downstairs and take back my bag of Twist. I'd do it tonight! I knew where they kept the candy—if there was any left. Maybe they'd eaten it all.

I looked at the counselors. Just then, one of them looked up at me and pointed. In a flash I pulled my head inside and shut the window. It sounded like they were laughing even louder down there. I didn't like it when grown-ups laughed at me. It was somehow worse than when kids did.

I lay in bed and listened until the night had really set in. It was quiet out there now. The counselors had all left in a couple of cars that had been waiting for them with their engines running. They hadn't come back yet.

Everyone in the dormitory was asleep. I got out of bed and tiptoed across the floor. Someone was snoring. I thought it was Sausage, but it wasn't because then he spoke.

"Where are you going, Kenny?" he whispered sitting up. It sounded like he was talking in his sleep.

"I'm just going downstairs to slit Matron's throat," I whispered back.

He let out a snicker.

"Go to sleep, Sausage."

I pushed the door open slowly. It was darker in the hall than inside the dormitory. It was the darkest time of night, but soon it would be daybreak again. Everything was still.

I crept along the wall to the stairs where I stopped and listened. I carried my *wakizashi* with me—a samurai never went anywhere without his short sword. You only carried your long sword when you went outside, and I was just going to the kitchen. At night, the samurai always kept both his swords under his pillow, but mostly I had to keep mine hidden under a floorboard in the dormitory.

I went down the stairs. A few of the steps creaked, but I knew which ones they were—I was a regular at this. I knew every corner of the whole place. It wasn't the first time I'd snuck around at night. That was the best time. If you knew how to do it right, it was like being invisible.

I stood downstairs between the girls' dormitories. In front of me was the mess hall. The curtains were drawn across the big windows, but you could see the trees swaying gently outside. I liked the big trees. They were larger than anything else around here and they always seemed to take it easy, even when they were swaying in a storm. They never showed any emotion, that they were angry or sad or happy. The trees were real samurai.

The kitchen was on my right. The door was open slightly and I tiptoed across the high threshold that was easy to trip over. Once last summer the cook had tripped over it with a pot of stew.

I stole quickly through the kitchen. The floor glowed in the moonlight that shone through the window like the beam from a flashlight. There was a cabinet at the very back where I suspected they kept the candy. I pulled at the handle, but the door was locked. I saw the keyhole, but no key.

"What are you doing here?"

In the silent kitchen, the voice felt like a karate kick. I hadn't heard anyone enter. I turned around and there was Matron. She had also tiptoed over the threshold. Maybe she had been spying on me the whole time. Maybe she snuck around like a ghost all night long.

"Children are not allowed in the kitchen," said Matron, "especially at night."

If you weren't allowed to be here, what difference did it make whether it was night or day?

"I lost my way," I said.

"You live upstairs," said Matron. "How could you end up down here?"

I don't live here at all, I thought to myself. *I'm imprisoned.*

"Tommy?"

Matron refused to say my samurai name.

"Answer me, Tommy."

"I think I was sleepwalking," I said.

"I've never noticed you doing that before."

"I've done it up in the dorm." I pointed upward as though

she didn't know where the dormitory was. "A few times."

"Nobody's said anything to me about it."

"I guess they didn't notice either."

"How did you notice it then, might I ask?" Matron bared her razor-sharp teeth in a smile of sorts. "If you were sleepwalking you'd hardly know about it, now would you?"

"I woke up once when I was on my way out of the dorm."

"But this time you didn't wake up until you were down here? Is that what you're trying to say?" She smiled again. "Or are you still asleep, Tommy?"

"I'm awake," I said and looked around. "I woke up in here."

"I see."

She didn't believe me, of course. She took a step forward. Her vampire face darkened when she moved out of the moonlight.

I felt my sword beneath my pajama top.

"What were you doing over by the cabinet?" she asked.

"What cabinet?" I turned back toward the cabinet instinctively.

"I'm sure you know what's in there," she said.

I didn't answer. The cabinet was no secret here at the camp.

"Then you also know that you only get candy at certain times," she said.

"It's . . . mine," I said.

"What did you say?" She took another step closer. I was

about to put up my arm to protect myself. I knew that she could hit you. "Repeat that."

"It's my candy," I said.

"Who said it wasn't?"

"I haven't gotten any of it."

"What? Any of *what*?"

"My bag of Twist."

"What is he talking about?" said Matron seeming to speak to somebody else.

"My mother brought me a bag of Twist."

"So?"

"I haven't had a single piece of it."

"What are you saying, Tommy? Are you standing there accusing us of stealing your bag of Twist?"

"I haven't had a single piece of it," I said again.

"I've never heard the like," said Matron. "Are you implying that we would steal from children?"

I didn't know what to say.

"We'll get to the bottom of this," said Matron as she took another step forward. "Out of my way!"

I jumped aside before she could put her hands on me. She stuck her hand down into the pocket of her dress and pulled out a key.

"We'll just see about this," she said, and she unlocked the cabinet door. It creaked as she opened it. She bent forward. "You can't see anything in here."

Matron walked over to one of the tables and turned on a lamp. When she went back to the cabinet, she looked even more horrible than before. The shadows made her look twice as tall and twice as fat.

She rummaged around among all the things inside there. I didn't want to look. There was the sound of rustling papers.

"Ha!" said Matron straightening up and peering down at me. "There's no bag of Twist in here!"

That's because you took it, I thought. But I didn't dare say it.

"How do you explain that, Tommy?"

"I know my mother had it with her," I said.

"Then maybe we should call your mother and check with her."

"We don't have a telephone," I said.

It was true. We'd never had one. Everybody had started getting telephones that year, but not us. They cost money.

"Maybe we should go there and ask her?"

"She's not home."

"Admit that you made the whole thing up, Tommy!"

There was no point in answering. There was no justice in this place—not at this camp. There was never any justice for children.

"Can I go now?" I asked.

"You mean continue walking in your sleep?" She laughed. "Can you find your way back up the stairs?"

I started to leave.

Quickly, she grabbed my shoulder. It hurt. I tried to twist free. Matron wasn't laughing anymore.

"I'm starting to get tired of you, Tommy," she said.

When I'd broken free of her grasp, she took hold of me again. With her other hand she twisted my ear. It hurt so much I thought she had twisted it clear off. It hurt all the way out to the ends of my hair. It hurt inside my head.

"Maybe we should send you home." She let go of my ear. "You don't seem to like it here anyway."

"I . . . like it here," I said as I tried to feel if my ear was still there.

I had to say that I liked it here. Not just because she was in the process of twisting my ear off, but because I had a plan. Only without the camp there was no plan.

"Really? You like it here? That's news to me."

I yawned, wider than I needed to.

"Can I go to sleep now?" I asked.

"Going to dream about the missing bag of Twist?"

I nodded.

"Go on up then. But don't let me catch you down here again after bedtime."

What was she doing down here herself in the middle of

the night? Stealing candy? Or drinking liquor? I thought she smelled of alcohol when she bent down over me. But that could have been something from the kitchen. The kitchen smelled strange.

I walked back through the mess hall and up the stairs. A seagull screeched from the lake. It sounded like a screech of terror.

"Where have you been?"

It was Sausage. He sat up in his bed when I entered the dorm.

"Shhh! You'll wake everyone," I whispered.

"I thought I heard someone say something down there."

"It was nobody," I said.

"So you didn't chop Matron's head off?" Sausage snickered.

"Not this time."

Sausage waved his hand. It was a small hand—about three times smaller than mine and three thousand times smaller than Matron's.

"Can't you sit here and talk for a while?" he whispered. "I can't sleep."

"We mustn't wake the others," I whispered back.

"Just for a little while, Kenny."

"Lie down and count sheep."

"I did that already. I managed seven hundred sheep heads."

"Like a real samurai," I whispered.

30

"Do you think I can become a real samurai, Kenny?"

"Tomorrow we can start working on your sword," I answered.

I moved closer to his bed. I didn't want the whole dormitory to wake up and cause Matron to come rushing up here and start shouting.

"Is it really true that the samurai preferred a wooden sword to a real sword, Kenny?"

"Some did."

"Why's that?"

"I already told you, Sausage."

"Tell me again."

"We can do it tomorrow. When we start making your sword."

"Does it take long? To make a sword?"

"We'll have to see. I don't know."

"Can't you tell me about that duel with the wooden sword? Or the wooden oar?"

"I've already told you, Sausage. Twice."

"Tell me again. I think I'll be able to sleep after that."

I sat on the edge of the bed. I wouldn't be able to get to sleep anyway until Sausage was asleep.

"It was a fight to the death," I began.

I told Sausage about the most famous duel between two samurais. In 1612, Miyamoto Musashi and Sasaki Kojiro, the two greatest warriors in Japan, faced each other. Musashi's mother died when she gave birth to him. When he was seven years old his father died too. His uncle, who was a priest, took care of him and raised him to be a samurai. When he was thirteen years old he killed his first adversary in a duel. It was a grown man, an experienced warrior. Three years later he defeated a real samurai. After that he left home for good. He roamed the country looking for other samurai to duel with. He had become a wave man.

"Why were they called wave men?" asked Sausage.

"Because they drifted around the countryside," I answered.

"And they fought with wooden swords?" asked Sausage.

"Most didn't," I said, "but Musashi did."

"What was it called again?"

"The wooden sword? It was called a *bokken*."

"That's what we're going to make for me, right?"

"Yes."

"The ones who had wooden swords used to beat the ones with steel swords, right?"

"Sometimes."

"Musashi preferred a wooden sword, didn't he?"

"Yes."

Sausage smiled. He acted like he was Musashi already just because he was going to get a wooden sword. He was childish, Sausage. He was ten years old, but sometimes he acted like he was four. Like now, when I sat here like his old man telling him a bedtime story.

"Keep going, Kenny!"

"No samurai in all of Japan had survived as many duels as Musashi," I said, "and when he met Kojiro he was twenty-eight years old."

"That's pretty old," said Sausage.

"No, no, he was still young."

"Okay."

"Kojiro came from one of the best sword-fighting schools," I continued, "and he had also defeated everyone he had ever faced in a duel."

"Otherwise he wouldn't have still been alive, right?" asked Sausage.

"That's right. Kojiro was considered the most formidable of all samurai. He almost seemed super-human. He was a master of the sword. Of course, it was a steel sword. His specialty was something they called "the Swallow" where he brought the sword down with such lightning speed that it was like a diving swallow."

"Wow!" said Sausage. You'd think he was hearing the story for the first time.

"He regarded Musashi as his greatest foe."

Sausage nodded. I could see him there in his bed almost as clearly as during the day. It got light quickly at the camp.

Soon it would be morning. Dragon Morning.

"It had been decided that the duel would be fought at the Hour of the Dragon," I continued. "That meant at eight o'clock in the morning. And when it was just a little before eight, Kojiro's men rowed him out to a narrow sandbank that lay between the two biggest islands of southern Japan. And there he waited for Musashi. There was a cold wind blowing. Minutes passed. Hours passed. But Musashi didn't show."

"I know what happened," said Sausage. "Musashi overslept."

"That's right," I said. "He barely had time to wash himself before he was driven down to the shore and rowed out to the sandbank. He was still sleepy and dozed off in the boat. He woke up with just enough time to carve himself a sword out of one of the oars."

"Neat!" said Sausage.

"Then he jumped ashore. Kojiro mocked him about the oar. But Musashi just pointed the oar at Kojiro's neck, and that was the signal that the duel had begun. They circled around each other. Both of them knew that one little mistake would mean death. And it was deathly silent too. The only sound you could hear was the waves washing against the shore and the screech of a few birds."

"Like here," said Sausage as he gestured with his arm to mean everywhere, "last night."

I had tried to see if I could hear any sounds from outside. There may have been the cry of a bird. But I couldn't hear any waves. The lake was calm last night.

"They stood there face to face," I continued, "and all of a sudden, Kojiro lunged with his sword."

"The Swallow," said Sausage.

"That's right, he did the Swallow. And at exactly the same split second, Musashi threw himself forward and brought his oar crashing down on Kojiro's head. They both stood there as if turned to stone. Seconds went by and no one who saw the duel could tell the outcome. Then a little gust of wind came and Musashi's headband was carried away with the breeze. It had been sliced in two. And Kojiro slowly began to sink to the ground."

"Dead!" said Sausage.

"Yes, stone dead. Musashi's oar had crushed Kojiro's skull. But in order for him to do that, Musashi had to move in just close enough for Kojiro to slice the headband from his forehead with his sword."

"But no closer!"

"Not even a hundredth of an inch closer," I said.

"His own sword was too short," said Sausage.

"Yes. Musashi needed something longer since Kojiro had the longest sword in all of Japan. But Musashi could not use another sword because Kojiro was the best when it came to judging the length of an opponent's sword. So Musashi knew that he would have an advantage if he got hold of a new weapon at the last second."

"The oar," said Sausage.

"It was perfect," I said, "perfectly calculated."

"Now I can sleep soundly," said Sausage.

4

ut I didn't sleep soundly. I hadn't in a long time. There was too much spinning around in my head. A few times I tried counting sheep, but that was even more boring than not being able to sleep. Janne, who slept three bunks away from me, talked in his sleep sometimes. Weird stuff like he was sailing on some kind of ship. It was always the same thing.

"Land ahoy!" he would shout out at three in the morning, imagining the whole camp was adrift at sea. Come to think of it, that wasn't far from the truth. The camp was sort of cut off from the rest of the world. The only time there was any contact was when the moms and dads came to visit.

To make it out of here to the big road, you had to move along secret paths through the forest, or follow the dirt road leading from the camp. But Matron sent out patrols whenever she thought someone was trying to escape.

We were planning an expedition through the woods anyway. We were going to make our way into town.

But first, the castle.

And before that, sleep. I turned over on my side for the zillionth time. Janne called out again like some lookout on a pirate ship, and I felt like getting up and going over to him and shouting, "Ship ahoy!" or something like that in his ear.

Sausage had asked Janne what he was dreaming about when he talked in his sleep, but he could never remember.

That was too bad because it seemed pretty fun to be sitting up in the mast bellowing away. A lot more fun than being here in our waking life.

I fell asleep right in the middle of that last thought. I dreamt.

A hand held out a bag to me and I looked down inside, where pieces of chocolate lay, only they were red.

I was standing in the lake rubbing water into my eyes so they would stay open. It wasn't a dream. I looked around and discovered that everyone else had already gone back up after the pretend morning wash. But I wasn't pretending. The water was cold and I kept on rubbing. I could feel how it ran down my back. Then I heard something behind me. I turned around and saw Kerstin. She didn't seem to be feeling cold.

"Isn't it cold?" she asked.

"Not after a while."

"Looks like you're trying to wash away something," she said.

"I'm washing away the sleep," I answered.

"What for?"

"You can't go around half-asleep all day."

"You can't?" It looked like she smiled. "Sounds pretty nice to me. Dream yourself away."

"You can do that at night," I said as I left the water and dried my face with the towel that had been lying in the grass.

"I have trouble sleeping here," said Kerstin. "There are too many people."

"Mm-hm."

"You think so too?"

"Yup. Especially grown-ups."

"We'd be able to manage without them," she said, looking sad, as though a cloud had just moved across the sun. I looked up at the sky, but there were no clouds. I rubbed my face again. This time it was to get dry.

"Pretty soon you'll have no skin left," said Kerstin.

I lowered the towel.

"Why are you here?" I asked. "Here at the camp? Now, this summer?"

"I don't know."

"Oh, come on."

"It was . . . so rowdy at home," she said, and looked away toward the main building and the playground that lay below the gable end. The smaller kids had started to swing and spin on the merry-go-round and play in the sand. Everyone seemed to be shouting at the same time.

"Yeah, plenty of peace and quiet out here," I said.

She looked back at me.

"It's not like you've got any choice," she said.

"That's where you're wrong," I answered.

The sun was in my eyes when I heard someone call my name. I was on my own in the lake. Kerstin had gone. It was Weine. He was another survivor from last summer. I didn't like him. He didn't like me.

Last summer we had fought without weapons. Neither of us had won, but neither of us had lost either. He wanted to be in charge, but he couldn't be in charge of me. This summer he had kept his distance. We hadn't spoken to each other even once. He had a small gang of flunkies who did everything he told them to. They weren't a proper unit—no band of warriors. They'd be useless in battle.

I blinked in the sun and saw him standing at the edge of the water. He said my name again with a special intonation that he obviously thought was funny.

"Hey, Ken-ny!"

I didn't answer. He called me Kenny and not Tommy. But it wasn't to be nice.

"Get yourself all clean now, Ken-ny?"

I didn't answer that either.

"Ever hear the one about the Japanese who mistook his toothbrush for a sword?"

"Ever hear about the idiot who got his face scrubbed with sand?"

"No. Is it about you, Ken-ny?"

I took a step toward him with my toothbrush in my hand.

"No weapons, we said!" He laughed after he said it. Then he gave a moronic salute, did an about-face, and marched off straight-legged in military style across the playground. I heard him laugh again. It sounded like a cackling seagull circling above the merry-go-round.

When Micke and Mats came up I was done brushing my teeth.

The toothpaste tasted awful and I tried to rinse away the taste with water from the lake, which didn't taste too good either.

I snorted and spit the water out.

"How's the soup?" asked Mats.

He was a little walleyed, and it looked like he was asking Micke as much as me.

"Better than cook's," I answered.

"And there's more of it," said Mats, looking out at the lake.

He could look left and right at the same time.

"Ever heard the story about the plane that crashed in the desert?" I asked.

They both shook their heads.

"The captain sent everyone out in search of food," I said. "When they came back, one of the flight attendants remarked they had good news and bad news. 'Let's hear the bad news first,' said the captain. 'All we found to eat is camel shit,' the flight attendant said. 'So what's the good news then?' 'There's plenty of it.'"

Mats laughed, but Micke didn't.

"What did he want?" he asked.

"You mean Weine? You saw him?"

Micke nodded.

"Nothing; he didn't want anything. Let's not talk about him. He's not worth it."

"So what did *she* want then?"

"What do you mean?" I wrapped the towel around my sword and started to walk back toward the main building. "What are you talking about?"

"That girl, whatever her name is. I saw you talking to her just now. What did she want?"

"Are you spying on me, Micke?"

"Cut it out, Kenny. You know you can't hide around here; you said so yourself. I just saw her—whatever her name is—speaking to you, that's all."

"Kerstin," I said. "Her name's Kerstin."

"She's from town," said Mats. "I've seen her there."

"Are you neighbors?" I asked.

"I've just seen her. She has a little sister, I think. But she's not here."

"What did she want?" Micke repeated.

"Have you become a parrot now, or what?" I asked.

"So you don't want to answer?"

"What's with up you, Micke?"

"Nothing's up with me. It's just . . ."

He didn't say any more.

"It's just what?" I asked.

"Just forget about it," said Mats and pulled Micke's arm.

"What are you doing?" shouted Micke. "Let go!"

"Take it easy," I said.

Micke grabbed at his sword.

"TAKE IT EASY!"

"He touched me," Micke muttered. "I've gotta defend my honor."

"You're in the same troop," I said. "He can touch you without you having to kill him."

"You're lucky I didn't have time to draw my sword," said

Micke, and he glared at Mats. Once a sword had been drawn from its scabbard, it had to be used; everyone knew that.

"Lucky for *you*," said Mats.

I had gathered the troop together and we were on our way into the woods when two of the counselors came up.

"Where are you going?" one of them asked but without directing her question at anyone in particular.

I kept on walking.

"We asked you where you're going, Tommy!"

I stopped but didn't answer.

"His name is Kenny," said Micke.

One of the counselors laughed.

"All right, *Kenny* then. Where are you heading?"

"Just out into the forest for a while."

"You're not thinking of running away, are you?" said the other counselor, who snickered too. "We were thinking of organizing a game of burnball," she continued. "You can't leave now. Then there won't be any good teams."

We looked at each other. It was a trick, of course. But we actually were the best. We'd been playing this kind of softball for years and could beat anybody.

There was a group of kids standing in the middle of the playing field in the distance.

They looked in our direction.

"We could forbid you to be in the forest," said the first counselor.

She was wearing tight shorts. You could see a few black hairs squiggling out onto her thighs.

"You've already done that, haven't you," I said.

It was often like that. We'd be about to do something, and then the counselors would show up.

All our plans were ruined. It was hard to think more than an hour ahead, and yet you had to do it.

We split up into teams. My troop was spread over two teams. They were mixed girls and boys. Kerstin was on my team. I was happy about that. She was quick and good at catching the ball in mid air.

Last week she caught a few that I'd hit when she was on the other team. She stood farther back than anyone else and waited. Everyone knew that I hit the farthest when I really connected with the ball, but she was the only one who realized just *how* far I could hit.

Sausage was ahead of me at the plate. On the third attempt, he got off a three-yard hit using the girls' flat bat. The ball rolled slowly into the grass. It was hard to imagine Sausage as a samurai right then. Or anytime. But he wanted to learn, and he was a loyal servant.

The word *samurai* comes from the Japanese word *saburau*

meaning "to serve." Sausage had already understood that. For others it could take a lifetime—however long or short that ended up being for a samurai. But at the same time, a short life for a samurai was a very long life for an ordinary person.

It was my turn at bat. I saw that Kerstin was standing up front at first base along with a few others who were waiting to run. They hadn't gotten anywhere yet. I tossed up the ball and waited as it reached its highest point. I concentrated on the ball. It was all in the concentration. The ball was the most important thing in my life at that moment. It hovered silently in the air and waited for me to decide when it was allowed to start to drop. My will was stronger than gravity.

I stood ready with the baseball bat. It was as long as a wooden sword, a *bokken*.

I held it like a samurai ready for battle: with both hands and with the blade angled upward.

I saw Kerstin and the others out of the corner of my eye. Everyone was motionless like the ball right now. They were in my control too. Nothing moved until I willed it.

I decided to let the ball drop. I lifted my sword and swung. The sword hit the ball's lower half exactly where I had aimed. That gave it more lift and spin, and before I'd even lowered the sword, the ball had disappeared so far up into the sky that you couldn't see it anymore. It had been swallowed up by the sun.

46

I knew it was my best hit ever. After a long moment, I let the sword fall to the ground where it transformed back into a bat.

Then I ran after the others. There was no hurry. That ball wouldn't come down before nightfall. But still, I ran as fast as I could. I wanted to catch up to Kerstin. I caught up to the others but not to her.

She was waiting for me by home plate. Everyone on the other team was still looking out for the ball. I waited for someone to shout, "Ball ahoy!" but nothing came.

Kerstin smiled at me.

"Now we're gonna win," she said.

Sausage stumbled in behind me.

"What a hit!" he said.

"I was lucky," I said. A samurai must never brag. It's a deadly sin. "Hit the ball at the right spot."

Kerstin smiled again. She seemed to know something about me that I knew too but had never told anyone. It was a strange feeling.

One of the counselors blew a whistle. It was time for what they passed off as food.

The worst thing about the meals in this place was that we got dessert three times a week. The dessert was fruit syrup soup or powdered pudding.

It was okay, but we were forced to eat it from the same plate we'd had our supper on, and since you could hardly eat the supper in the first place, it was even worse once it got mixed with the dessert.

Today we had pig's liver and boiled potatoes for supper. I had put a lot of effort into training myself to eat whatever was put in front of me, but sometimes it was hard. The worst part was trying to eat with so many people around you. It was against the samurai rules. You were only allowed to eat in a big group when the samurai gathered for battle. Otherwise you were supposed to eat alone or together with just one other samurai.

The most important food for a samurai was rice. They had served us rice only once this summer, and that had been boiled in snot. If the camp cook had entered the world championship of disgusting cooking, she would have won as easy as pie. Sometimes she would look out from the kitchen to see for herself how many of us she was torturing at the two long tables. Then she'd go back inside and prepare dinner for Matron and the counselors and herself: pork chops, grilled fish, a baked potato, and ice cream. We could smell it. And chocolates from a bag of Twist, with coffee.

One of the counselors set down a pot of fruit-syrup soup at our table and started to ladle it onto our dishes that still contained scraps of liver. The soup looked like nosebleed mixed with little white worms. The blood was thin like it had been filched from someone who was already anemic; the worms were grains of tapioca and tasted like boogers. Or maybe the other way around.

The slimy tapioca grains were used in almost every dessert. They must have gotten a deal on them at some market for reject cattle feed.

I looked down at my plate. I had tried to eat some of the potato, but it had gotten sticky and wet from the sauce.

The bits of liver looked like leather.

The counselors approached with the pot of soup.

"Aren't you going to eat up?" Sausage asked and looked at my plate. He had even licked his plate so that it would be clean for the dessert. You really had to admire him.

"I don't know what I'm going to do," I said.

Once I poured everything onto the floor under the table. I acted like I'd knocked the plate over by accident.

But the counselors had looked at me suspiciously.

"You can't chuck it on the floor again," said Sausage. "They'll kill you."

"I could say you did it," I said, and I reached for Sausage's gleaming plate. It shone like a beacon as the sunlight broke through the window and hit it.

Sausage tightened his grip on the plate. He looked scared.

"W-would you really do that, Kenny?"

"I was only joking," I said as I pulled my hand back.

Sausage looked at me like he didn't quite believe it.

"You know I wouldn't be able to do something like that, Sausage."

They had reached us with their pot of fruit slop. Sausage held out his plate.

"I don't want any dessert," I said.

"You haven't finished your dinner," said one of the counselors.

"I'm still eating."

"You have to eat up your food, Tommy." She nodded at the pot. "Otherwise you don't get any dessert."

"I said I don't want any."

I raised my head and looked at her. She didn't look retarded. She smiled a strange smile, knowing she was annoying me.

"I really want to take my time eating this delicious liver stew," I said. "I really want to enjoy the taste."

"When we come back you'd better have eaten everything," she said, and the smile was gone.

"What are you gonna do now, Kenny?" asked Sausage when the counselors had headed off down the table looking for fresh victims.

"Enjoy the food," I said.

"How?" asked Sausage and laughed.

"Well, it's got nothing to do with the taste anyway," I said. "Slide your plate over, Sausage."

"What?" He looked down at the red goop on his plate. "What do you want it for?"

"Just give it here," I said, and I scraped the liver from my plate onto Sausage's.

Once the surface had settled, it was hidden under the soup. My plate was clean.

I slid Sausage's plate back.

"What am I supposed to do now?" he asked.

"One thing at a time," I said.

"I wanted that soup," said Sausage.

"You've still got it."

"But I don't want any more liver," he said.

"Just tell the counselors there were pieces of liver in the dessert," I said.

"Will they believe that?"

"No."

"Now you're being mean, Kenny."

He looked like he was about to cry, knowing he would get the punishment that was meant for me. But I wasn't the type to let someone else take my punishment.

"I don't want to get blamed for everything," Sausage continued.

"Pass your plate," I said, and nodded toward the far end of the table where the counselors had already been with their slop pot. Everyone seemed to have already forced down their liquid blood pudding. The plates were fairly white with red splotches here and there.

Sausage looked around. Then he whispered something to the guy sitting to his right. They exchanged plates, and with that, Sausage's plate began to make its way down the table. I turned around to see if the cook or Matron or any of the counselors were watching, but the only grown-ups in the room right now were the counselors serving up the soup, and they were way at the other end of the mess hall.

Finally, the plate made it to the end of the table. It was in front of a girl named Ann. Ann had brown hair and a turned-up nose that made her look a little stuck-up, but I don't think she was. She looked surprised, but she must have realized what was coming. She had seen the plate making its way to the end of the table.

We watched as she stood up, holding Sausage's plate, and walked the length of the table, down to the end where the counselor was almost done ladling out the soup. I didn't see if she said anything to the counselor, and I couldn't hear anything from where I was sitting.

Sausage couldn't hear either. He looked nervous. I felt

strange. I hadn't intended for anything to happen to that girl. I didn't even know she was the one sitting at the end of the table, but it was Sausage or her.

The counselor nodded. Ann turned and walked back.

She came toward us and I expected her to set the plate down in front of us, but she didn't even look at us—not at Sausage or me. She just continued on into the kitchen and came back without the plate. She sat back down at her place as if nothing had happened.

"What did she say to the counselor?" asked Sausage.

I didn't answer. I checked to see if Ann was looking in our direction, but she didn't seem to be looking in any particular direction.

"So, you managed to finish your supper after all, Tommy."

I heard the counselor's voice close to my ear. It felt like she wanted to burst my eardrum.

"But now there's no more dessert," she said.

"Too bad," I said.

"I would have liked to have had some," said Sausage.

"You've already had your portion," said the counselor.

"I have no—" the numbskull started to say, and I kicked him in the shin.

"Ow!"

"What is it?" asked the counselor.

"N-nothing," said Sausage. "Maybe a mosquito."

"There aren't any mosquitoes in here," said the counselor, waving her hand.

"Now let's thank the Lord for our food," said the other counselor, and we stood up.

"THANK YOU, LORD, FOR OUR FOOD. AMEN!"

We were allowed to leave the table. Thank you, Lord, for our food. Half of us died; the rest just . . . spewed.

———————+———————

There was a canoe floating on the lake, but it was so far out that you couldn't see whether anyone was sitting in it. We were just having our evening wash. Some splashed themselves with murky water. Some didn't. Ann was standing thirty feet out. Kerstin was standing next to her. They were looking at the canoe that was gliding farther and farther away. I waded over to them. There weren't many kids still down by the lake. Soon they would make us go to bed. The sun hadn't set yet, but we were forced to go to bed. One thing I knew for sure: when I grew up I would never go to bed before the sun.

Kerstin and Ann saw me coming.

"That canoe looks abandoned," I said, and nodded out toward the lake.

"You can't tell," said Kerstin.

"Thanks for the plate," said Ann.

"So you saw it was me?"

"Didn't everybody?"

"Not the counselors."

"They saw the plate," she said.

"I didn't mean for you to get caught."

"I didn't get caught, did I?"

"What did you say to her, anyway?"

Ann looked at Kerstin. Kerstin looked at me.

"We could tell you," said Kerstin, "but on one condition."

"Oh, yeah?"

"That Ann gets to see the castle too."

5

It was too late to go see any castles tonight. To be honest, there wasn't really any castle to see. There were plans for a very fine castle. There was a foundation and a nearly finished moat. And there were walls that were being built, but they weren't even half finished. Sometimes I doubted that we'd get the castle finished before the end of the summer, but I didn't dare tell anyone—not Sausage, not Micke or Lennart or Janne or Sven-Åke or Mats. Not Kerstin. Or Ann. What would I say to them?

Why had Kerstin told Ann about the castle? I actually hadn't dared ask. Maybe it had to do with the plate of fruit slop. Maybe this was a way of getting back at me somehow.

It wasn't easy to understand how girls' minds worked, and yet . . . well, this summer it had become a little more interesting to find out how a girl's mind worked. Or what a girl had to say.

If someone had told me that a year ago, I would have laughed at them. Or punched them out on the spot.

The sun was finally gone from the new night. There were four big windows in the dormitory and they all showed the same sky that had darkened but not become really black. I sat up and saw the moon. It wasn't a half moon, but more like a sliver. Like a *katana*, the long sword. The tip was pointing straight down toward the forest. Toward the castle.

I sat there in bed. Janne mumbled something in his sleep, but I didn't hear what it was. Something from the sea. Otherwise, everything was quiet. Quiet. This was the time when I would think—think intently about nothing. That was the path to total self-control. But it was only possible at night, when the only things that broke the silence were sleepwalkers and sleeptalkers.

But tonight I couldn't think about nothing. All I could think about right now was girls—what they were like. Then I thought about what they turned into. I thought about Matron and the camp counselors. What did Kerstin think about them? What did Ann think? It must be awful to grow up and become like that.

Anything was better than that.

I thought about Mama. She had been a girl once. In her case, that wasn't so hard to imagine. But Matron? And the counselors?

Then I thought about how I was going to grow up one day too. I couldn't wait, but at the same time it scared me. What would I be like? Who would I become? I hoped that I wouldn't turn into somebody else. But one thing I knew for sure: it wouldn't be easy to continue being a samurai in this country once I was a grown-up. There was a chance they might think I was crazy and put me away in an asylum. Camp for the rest of my life.

There was someone I knew who was just barely grown up. Or he'd stopped growing up just when he was about to become an adult. Like something bad had happened to him. I had met Matron's son last summer. He was eighteen or nineteen and his name was Christian. He hadn't said much. When he looked at Matron, he seemed scared. When he looked at me, he seemed strange. There was something about his eyes that had frightened me.

I had seen him wandering around the grounds after sundown. Something about his hands looked . . . sinister. He clenched his fists and opened them again. Maybe he'd be visiting this summer too. He used to come for a week or so every summer. He had a moped. This summer he said he'd be coming by car.

I slipped out of bed and walked over to one of the windows. The moon blade was still pointing straight down at the castle that was hidden in the forest. It was a sign that maybe I ought to understand. The forest started right where the gates to the camp ended. The trees formed a wall, but I knew how to get through that wall and into the forest beyond.

The glowing blade slowly started to sink down toward the forest. It wanted to show me something—to get me to understand that I should go to the castle. Now. Tonight. There was something waiting for me there.

A gentle wind blew across the grounds below the dormitory. I looked up at the windows in our room and saw something white. It was moving. Maybe one of the counselors had seen me. Or worse yet, Matron. If she had, I wouldn't get away this time. I heard a window open. It was a penetrating noise in the darkness. I saw the white thing transform into a face. It was Sausage. I waved to him to keep quiet, close the window, and go back to bed. All of that was in the wave.

It was too difficult for him to understand everything. He didn't say anything, which was lucky, but he waved back and shut the window. Three minutes later, as I was almost to the edge of the forest, I saw him crawl across the grounds like a snail, pass through the gates, get up, and come over to me.

"Damn it, Sausage!"

"Where are you going, Kenny? Are you running away?"

"Keep your voice down."

"You keep *your* voice down."

He gestured at the forest. It was dark like the inside of a cave in there. No light seemed to penetrate, not even the moonlight that still shone out here. Sausage's face looked blue in the glow, like war paint.

"Are you going to run away this time?"

"Go back to bed," I whispered. "They could have seen you."

"Then the chances of that will be even bigger if I go back."

"You can't come with me."

"Why not?"

"It's dangerous."

"Then you need my help." He slapped his hand on his hip. His little sword hung at his side. We hadn't made Sausage's big sword yet. He looked around. His face was covered in shadows. No more war paint. He looked older, too, like his own big brother, if he'd had one.

"What's so dangerous?" he asked.

I looked toward the main camp building. We couldn't stand here any longer. Someone could look out the window at any moment and see us. We would be easy to spot where

we were standing—white against the black forest. Maybe
Matron could see us.

I pointed at the forest and walked in among the trees.
Sausage walked two steps behind me. I could hear his
breathing. It sounded like he had run four times around all
the bases in burnball. He was scared. I was a little scared
myself. His fear must have infected me. And now I had to
look out for him. I had to make sure he made it back to the
dormitory in one piece.

The moat seemed wider at night. I looked up and the glowing
sword was still suspended there, right above our heads. It
hadn't moved farther off like the moon usually does when
you come closer. The castle lay in a glade. It was lighter here
than among the trees, but it was still dark.

"We've never been here at night before," said Sausage.

I didn't answer. I was trying to see if there was anything
out of place.

"It looks bigger than it does during the day," said Sausage.

"Quiet!"

"What is it, Kenny?" He looked around and stood closer
to me. "Did you hear something?"

I moved closer to the moat—or the ditch, rather, since
there was no water in it yet. I bent down. It looked like

footprints in the dirt. Big footprints. Sausage bent down next to me.

"See something?" I asked.

"Could be boots," he said.

"Size twelve," I said, "or bigger."

"Did someone that big find our castle?"

"Looks that way."

"Matron?"

"The size fits, anyway," I said.

"So what do we do?"

"Nothing," I said. "We don't do anything 'til we know something."

"We have to investigate, don't we?"

"Yes."

I walked cautiously across the bottom of the moat, up the other side, and across the outer courtyard. There weren't any footprints there; the ground was hard. I climbed over the inner stone wall. We had lugged the rocks through half the forest to build it. Once we had finished building the workshops and warriors' quarters on top of the wall, no one would be able to make it over. Not even a giant with a size-twelve boot.

A forest bird's shriek startled us like a warning call. We stopped short behind the wall of the inner courtyard. So far, only one of the side towers had a roof. It was built out of earth and twigs and pine branches. We had barely started on the main tower. The bird shrieked again.

"Let's go back," said Sausage.

"You wanted to come along."

"That was . . . before."

"Do you want to be a warrior or not?" I asked. "Or was that just before too?"

Sausage mumbled something I couldn't hear. The bird shrieked a third time—a shorter call. It was cut short, like someone had chopped its head off in mid-screech.

"It's only a bird."

"Maybe it saw something."

"It saw *us*," I said, and continued toward the towers. "It got nervous."

Sausage waited behind me. I walked slowly around the first guard tower, then around the second. I passed a side tower. Then I stood on the floor of the main tower. There was nothing here. We were alone in our castle.

I went back to Sausage.

"There's nobody here but you and me," I said.

"But what about the footprints?"

"They must have been left by someone who walked through here yesterday. A hunter maybe."

"What if he comes back?"

"I don't think he will."

"Maybe he'll tell everyone."

"Why would he do that?"

I turned around to face the castle. I tried to see it like a grown-up would.

"He didn't even realize what it was. All he saw was a hut, if he even saw that much."

"If Matron finds out, she'll come here and destroy it," said Sausage.

"She won't find out," I said.

"But what if she does, Kenny?"

I didn't answer. I didn't want to think about Matron when I was in the castle.

"What if?" Sausage repeated.

"Then there will be war."

The moon blade had grown fainter once we were back in the dorm, as though someone was slowly rubbing out the light with a rag. Soon the sun would rise again. This summer it always rose.

Nobody saw us as we snuck back up to the dorm. Not that we noticed anyway.

Were the footprints a sign? Was that what the moon

wanted to show me? Was it even a footprint at all? We would have to examine it in daylight.

I closed my eyes. I must have fallen asleep. I dreamt something, but whatever it was, I had forgotten it by the time I woke up.

After the morning wash, I remembered it. The cold water on my head perked me up and I could think clearly, and the sun in my eyes quickly brought me back from the kingdom of sleep.

I had dreamt that I was riding in a car with my dad. We had never had a car, and I didn't have a father anymore, so it was definitely a dream—especially since I was the one driving. We were going really fast, but I never saw any sign of a road. It was just sky and pastures. When I turned the wheel, the car followed just as smooth as silk. It was like flying. I hadn't ever done that either. "You're doing just fine," said Papa. "Where should we go?" I asked. "Out of here, just out of here," he answered. So we got out of there, just out of there. High above lakes, fields and tractors, over treetops.

All of a sudden, we were parked in front of a castle. It was ours and it was finished. It was almost an exact copy of the powerful Matsumoto castle from the 1500s. There were several smaller towers that together formed a main tower. "I've been here," said Papa. "You have?" I asked. "Didn't you see my footprints?" he answered.

"Should we go look at the footprint now?" Sausage was done with his pretend washing. He waved at the sky with his unused toothbrush. "It might rain and then the footprint will be washed away."

The sky was blue, just like the sky I'd driven the car through. I hadn't noticed what kind of car it was in my dream. I hoped it was American. A new Ford Thunderbird.

"There won't be any rain this summer."

"But shouldn't we head over there?"

"Gather the troop," I answered.

Sausage's face lit up like the sun. It was the first time he had been assigned that task.

We marched out to the edge of the forest behind the building. There wasn't going to be any burnball today. And I didn't want Kerstin to see us either, or Ann. I didn't know how I'd be able to explain them to the rest of the troop. I still hadn't solved that problem.

The glade looked like it did last night, only lighter. Not a lot of sun made it down here. That was why we had chosen it. From thirty feet away you could hardly even tell there was a glade.

Sausage led us to the moat. He had been along last night after all. It was only fair.

"There it is!" he said and pointed at the ground. "See it?"

"No," said Micke.

He looked annoyed. He must have thought that he wasn't ranked second after me anymore, that Sausage had been given that position. But if Micke couldn't understand that it was just for now, just for this short moment, then maybe he wasn't cut out to be a samurai lord, a *daimyo*. A *daimyo* has to understand several things at once. Understand that things change, and change back.

"Of course you can see it," I said. "It's a boot print."

"Mm-hm," said Lennart.

"Whose could it be?"

That was Janne.

"It's a big one," said Sven-Åke.

"Must be a man's," said Lennart.

"Or Matron's," said Mats.

Janne let out a laugh.

"Not even she would dare come out here in the middle of the night."

Sausage looked proud when Janne said that.

"Probably some farmer who got lost."

That was Micke.

"In the middle of the night?" asked Lennart.

"Day or night makes no difference to them," said Micke.

"What, like a sleepwalker, you mean?" said Janne.

"Farmers plow day and night," Micke continued, ignoring Janne. "It's light all the time."

"Only right now they're taking in the hay," said Lennart.

"They haven't been doing any plowing anyway." Janne looked around. "And there's no hay here either."

"It could have been a hunter," said Sausage.

"Anyway, he's not here now," said Micke.

"He might come back," said Sausage.

"Then he'll lose his head," said Micke.

"Gotta be a big one," said Sven-Åke, "judging by his shoe size."

"Who cares?" said Micke. "So much the better."

"How many heads have you collected so far, Micke?" asked Lennart.

"What do you mean by that?" said Micke. He spun around toward Lennart.

"How many heads have you chopped off so far?"

"Thirty-eight, counting yours," Micke answered and grabbed at his sword.

"Stop it!" I shouted.

Micke hadn't managed to pull out his sword yet.

"You can fight later," I said. "Right now we've got a lot of work to do."

Half the troop was out in the forest collecting fir branches and brush. The other half was working on the inner wall. There was plenty of stone. All you had to do was dig a little and you found some. Beyond this part of the forest there were fields surrounded on all sides by stone fences. They were like walls. You would have thought there wouldn't be any rocks left after the farmers had built all those walls, but there seemed to be tons of them still in the ground.

If stones had been worth something, we'd all have been rich. But none of us knew what it was like to be rich—no one here at this camp. This was a place for poor people. You only had to speak to anyone here for half a minute to realize that. You just had to look at the moms and dads who came and visited once every summer, if they came at all. And none of them came in a Ford Thunderbird. Hardly anybody came in a car at all. Most of them walked from the turn-off and huffed and puffed their way through the front gate, just as drenched in sweat as Mama had been.

Janne didn't have a mom or a dad. Not that he lived with, anyway. He had been living at an orphanage and now he was here. Then he was going to be sent to live with a foster family that he hadn't even met yet. They had a farm up north somewhere.

"You'll probably get to drive a tractor," said Sausage when Janne told us.

Janne nodded but didn't say anything.

"Maybe they've got horses," Sausage continued.

"If they don't, they're not really farmers," said Sven-Åke.

"Do they have any kids?" asked Mats.

Janne just shrugged.

"Then you'd have brothers and sisters," Mats continued.

"I've already got brothers and sisters," said Janne, and walked off.

Just when I was thinking about that, Janne came back into the glade with an armful of fir branches. It seemed like my thoughts had made him come back. He laid the branches on the ground and walked up to me.

"Do you really think we'll get the castle finished before the end of the summer, Kenny?"

"Of course," I answered.

He looked like he doubted it.

"We get to decide when it's finished."

"And then what?" He opened his arms wide and said, "Then we've gotta leave all this. Just when we're done, we have to leave it."

"That's true for all samurai," I said. "You've gotta leave the castle sometimes."

"But they come back, Kenny."

He turned to me again. He looked me right in the eye. We were the same height. I wondered if we'd still be the same height when we were grown up.

I can't remember how tall my dad was compared to other grown-ups, and Janne had no idea what his dad looked like.

"We're never coming back." He pointed with his hand again. "The castle's just going to stand there and rot."

"There'll be other summers."

"Not for us, Kenny. You know that."

"Yeah."

"We'll be too old next summer."

I didn't answer.

"This is the last summer," he continued. "The last samurai summer."

"There will be others after us," I said. "Sausage will be coming back and so will Sven-Åke and Mats."

"Yeah, yeah. But for us it's over."

"Camp, maybe, but not everything else."

"What do you mean 'everything else?'"

"There will always be another summer. And you'll still be a samurai."

Just as I said that, I heard a distant rumbling in the sky.

We looked up but didn't see anything. Then the airplane appeared. It was gliding along, right above the glade, like an eagle. It was on its way to secret places, new places. I thought about my dream. I was imagining myself sitting up there looking down at myself. Big Kenny looking down at little Kenny.

"I'd like to become a pilot," said Janne. We were still gazing upward even though the plane was gone now. The rumbling from the engines lingered in the sky like thunder. The airplane was a thunderbird. A Thunderbird.

"Go ahead and become one then," I said.

"On a farm?" He lowered his head and looked at me. "I'll be lucky if I get to drive a tractor."

"That's pretty good," I said.

"A tractor isn't an airplane."

Don't be so sure about that, I thought, and I remembered my dream again.

"I may not even get to drive the tractor," said Janne in a low voice. "Besides, maybe they don't even have one."

Now we heard a different kind of rumbling as a few of the troop entered the glade with more branches.

"I don't want to leave the castle," said Janne. He looked me in the eye again. "I mean after the summer."

"No," I said. "Who does?"

"But they're gonna force us." He waved his hand, this time toward the camp.

"Matron. The counselors."

I didn't answer.

"If they didn't exist . . ." said Janne and fell silent.

I waited.

"If there weren't a camp at all then we could stay on here. As long as we wanted."

I still said nothing. I thought about him and how it would be for him to arrive at the strangers' farm for the first time. At least I had a mother.

"Right?" he continued. "If it didn't exist?"

"But it does," I said and nodded. "It's over there behind the trees."

You couldn't see it from here, but you didn't have to go more than a few hundred yards through the forest before you could make out the closest building.

"But what if . . ." he said.

What if there were no "if?" I thought. Maybe you could take away the "if." If there were no camp. If it didn't exist at all . . . There is no camp. It doesn't exist at all.

I looked around. The entire troop was assembled. Everyone was working on the castle. Everyone looked strong.

We could do it.

It was Janne who had said it, but I had probably just been waiting for someone to say what was already in my head, inside my brain.

If there were no camp, then we could stay on here. As long as we wanted. If there were no grown-ups telling us what to do anymore.

6

It was morning again. The sun rose on good and evil alike. This morning, the evil had cooked up something new. Anyone who didn't eat everything on their plate would get it back the next time they sat down at the table. No one would get a fresh helping until they'd eaten the old one. There had been cold oatmeal and blue milk in my dish. When it was taken back to the kitchen, the oatmeal was even colder and the milk bluer still. I hadn't even lifted the spoon.

"You know what's coming, Tommy," said the counselor when she went off with the dish.

I didn't answer. The oatmeal wouldn't taste any better or worse in the morning or in the evening. The milk would probably go sour, but I actually preferred sour milk. But I wouldn't eat that either. I was never going to eat it. It was like the start of a new battle. I looked around the mess hall but differently than I had before. I seemed to be seeing everything through new eyes. I had become someone else—someone who was even more unlike the boy who had once been Tommy.

The sun burned our eyes. We stood lined up on the grounds in two columns. We were going to march around the lake to the big swimming area on the other side. They called it a swimming trip, but I called it a swimming trek. The counselors kept a close eye on us from both sides. When the smaller kids got tired we had to carry them.

We marched. The lake glittered to the right through the trees. The ground smelled good. The smell of the forest was my favorite smell. With it filling my nostrils, I felt like a free warrior. Well, not right then, of course, walking in line but otherwise.

All of a sudden, I tripped on a root, fell, and slammed into the ground.

A few choice words flew out of my mouth.

Someone giggled behind me. I quickly jumped up and turned around.

"What did you do that for?" It was Kerstin.

"Do what?"

"Throw yourself to the ground?"

I saw that she was just kidding around so I started walking

again. She took two quick steps and started walking next to me.

"Why do you swear so much?" she asked.

"I don't swear much."

"Really?"

"I used to do it a lot more."

"Wow. You must have had a really foul mouth."

"It's not always bad to swear," I said.

"Oh yeah?"

"Sometimes there are no other words you can use."

"Thou shalt not swear," said Kerstin. "It says so in the Bible."

"Mm-hm."

"One of the Ten Commandments."

"Thou shalt not force children to eat pig swill," I said.

"What's that?"

"That's worse," I said. "Worse than swearing."

"I mean, is that a commandment too?"

She smiled. When the sun hit her eyes they got lighter. They turned a different color—green almost.

"You bet. One of the most important ones."

"Do you know any more?"

"Thou shalt not steal a kid's bag of Twist," I said.

"I don't get it."

"It doesn't matter."

"Sure it does," she said. "I can hear that it does."

Before long we had marched around half the lake. In a while we'd be able to see the big swimming area. The rays from the sun transformed the water into silver, and I could see a sailboat out on the lake. The sail was as white as our sheets the night before the moms and dads came to visit.

"What, did somebody steal a bag of Twist from you?" asked Kerstin. "You had a whole bag of Twist?"

I didn't answer.

"It sucks if you can't say it," she said.

"Now who's got a foul mouth?"

"Hmm."

"Okay, my mom brought me a bag of Twist and they took it."

"They? Who's 'they'?"

"The grown-ups."

"Are you sure about that?"

One of the counselors appeared alongside us. She had probably been eavesdropping from behind and wanted to hear more.

"You're moving too slowly," she said. "The line isn't staying together." I looked up and saw that we'd fallen fifteen feet behind those ahead of us. I picked up the pace and so did Kerstin. Her stride was bigger than mine. Her legs were longer.

"Did they really steal it?" she asked. "Would they really do something so awful?"

"It's gone," I answered. "I didn't get one single piece."

"Maybe it's been forgotten somewhere," she said.

"A forgotten bag of Twist? You believe that?"

"No." She smiled again.

"Shouldn't that be one of the Ten Commandments?" I continued. "Thou shalt not steal a kid's bag of Twist."

"That's included in the other one," she said. "Thou shalt not steal."

"It should have its own commandment."

"Have you asked them?"

"I've even looked for it," I answered and told her the story.

"Weren't you scared?" asked Kerstin after I'd finished telling her.

She looked scared herself as though Matron had suddenly appeared and was standing there panting right next to us.

We were approaching the swimming area. I could hear children shouting all across the wide bay as they swam.

The jetties extended far out into the water. I could see the ends of them sticking out beyond the rocks that we were going to round in a minute. It might have been a nice place to swim, but I had never been able look at it like a real beach where you went to have fun. I was never going to come here once I could decide for myself. There were many places I had no intention of ever going back to.

"Weren't you scared?" asked Kerstin again.

"Of course I was scared."

"She didn't try to hit you?"

"No. Lucky for her."

I didn't want to saying anything about how Matron had tried to twist my ear off. I was ashamed of it. I thought about how I had to make sure I didn't touch my ear. Then Kerstin might notice that it was still swollen.

I looked at her but she wasn't looking at my ear. She seemed to be gazing out across the lake toward the camp, as though she could see Matron standing on the steps.

"She's creepy."

"Worse than that," I said.

"Next time you do something, maybe you'll get sent home."

"There's nobody at home," I said.

"Why not?"

"My mom's away."

"To some other camp then?"

"I don't think there's anyone who wants me," I said.

"LISTEN UP!" shouted one of the counselors.

There was a light breeze blowing at the end of the dock. I could see that there was a little wind in the sail of the boat that was still drifting around aimlessly in the middle of the lake. It seemed that it was looking for a way out but couldn't find one because the lake was too big. The boat was stuck there for good.

"What were you talking to her about?" asked Sausage.

He was sitting next to me. When he was only wearing swimming trunks he really looked like a sausage. A breakfast sausage, thicker than a hot dog.

"What did she want?"

"Nothing."

"I saw you talking to her. You sure talked a long time for it to be nothing."

"She just happened to be walking next to me."

"We said no girls."

"We did?"

"You're the one who said it, Kenny."

"That all depends on what you mean."

"Well, what do you mean then?"

"Nothing," I said because I didn't want to talk about it. "Wanna dive in?"

We dove in. The water was clearer here than over by the camp. I could see my fingers in front of me. They were green. Green like Kerstin's eyes. I thought of her again. It was Sausage's fault. I could see his legs wiggling in front of me like two small, stubby cocktail sausages. I stayed below the surface until it felt like my head was going to explode. And yet, it wasn't that I thought I couldn't breathe. It was that, for a moment, I felt I wanted to stay down there.

I gasped for air when I came up.

"I thought you'd drowned," said Sausage.

"A new record."

Sausage climbed up the ladder.

"I think it's snack time," he said.

The snack consisted of cinnamon buns and diluted fruit concentrate. Everybody got some except me.

"You didn't finish your oatmeal, Tommy," said the counselor.

"Where is it?" I asked.

They hadn't brought it along. If they had, I would have eaten it up just to show them.

I went and sat behind the big rock.

The sailboat was still out there, but the wind had died down. The sail hung limply like a bed sheet.

"Here."

I looked up. Kerstin held out a paper cup.

"Then there won't be any for you," I said.

"I took a second cup," she said.

"So drink it then."

"You don't have to play tough. Not in front of me."

"I'm not thirsty," I said.

"You will be. We've got to walk back too."

She held the cup even closer to me. I took it and drank. The fruit concentrate was weak, but it didn't matter.

"You can have half of my bun if you want," she said.

"I'm not hungry."

"You didn't eat any breakfast."

"You call that breakfast?" I asked.

She sat down. I moved over slightly. She held her hand over her eyes and gazed out at the lake.

"That boat's not moving," she said.

"There's no wind."

"What's your favorite breakfast?" she asked.

"Rice."

"Rice? You mean boiled rice?"

"Yeah."

"Is that what you usually have for breakfast?"

"No. Not here."

"At home then? Do you usually eat boiled rice at home?"

"Uh . . . no."

"But it's still your favorite breakfast?"

"It's a samurai breakfast," I said.

"Doesn't sound very good."

"That's not the point."

She didn't answer. She seemed to be thinking about what I had said, but I wasn't sure because I couldn't see her eyes.

You have to see someone's eyes to know what they're thinking.

"My favorite is ham and eggs," she said without lowering her hand from her eyes. She was still gazing out at the sailboat. "And jam on toast."

"Yeah, I've heard about that," I said. "Do you get that when you're home?"

"On Sundays." She lowered her hand and looked at me. "Sometimes."

"Maybe you can put in an order with the cook for Sunday," I said and got up and walked back to the others.

My head felt strange. I turned around. Kerstin was still sitting by the rock. Maybe she was keeping an eye on the sailboat. While I had been sitting there, I'd thought about how you can go just as far in a sailboat as you can in an airplane—even with that boat, if you could get it out of the lake. Anywhere in the world. That boat might be able to sail from this puny little puddle all the way to Japan. The sail had caught some wind now—wind that might have blown in all the way from the sea. The boat looked like it was about to take to the air.

"Hi there, Romeo!"

I turned around again.

"Aren't you going to take your girl back with you, Romeo? Are you just going to leave her all alone by the rock?"

It was Weine.

"What's her name?"

"None of your business."

"Maybe I should go ask her myself."

Weine had two other guys with him. They stood behind him and snickered whenever he said anything. I didn't understand why.

"Go ahead," I heard from behind me. Seemed like everyone was talking behind me today. I turned around. It was Kerstin.

"Go ahead and ask me then," she said and looked straight at Weine.

Weine's face looked dumber than usual.

"Forgotten how to speak?" asked Kerstin.

You could see the wheels turning inside Weine's skull. I was a spectator watching from the sidelines, even though I was standing right between them.

"Aw, what the hell," said Weine, and he started walking back toward the beach.

His gang looked at him for a moment before following him.

Kerstin stood next to me.

"Guess he didn't want to know my name after all."

"He's an idiot."

"You shouldn't say that about people." She looked at me. "There are real idiots you know. People who can't help it."

"Sure, there's one right over there," I said, and I nodded

toward Weine who was walking quickly across the narrow strip of sand. The other two stumbled after him.

"No," Kerstin smiled, "he's just stupid."

I laughed. It felt good. She was sharp. You had to be on your toes with her. Weine didn't stand a chance. And yet it was only words.

I couldn't see Sausage anywhere and no one else had seen him either. I asked but nobody knew.

"I think he was going to do some diving over on the other side," said Micke. "But that was a while ago."

There was a jetty on the opposite side of the headland where the water was deeper. Anyone who wanted to do real diving had to go over there. Once Sausage had learned to dive, that was all he ever wanted to do. He had become more daring. He'd throw himself way out.

The counselors had just said that it was time to get our things together and march back to the penitentiary. The sun had begun to go down.

I started to walk toward the other side of the headland.

"Where are you going, Tommy?"

Normally I wouldn't have answered, but this time I turned around.

"Sausage isn't here. I'm going to get him."

"His name isn't Sausage." The counselor had put her hands on her hips. "He's hardly a sausage is he?"

I had a bad feeling that something had happened to him.

"Run and fetch him then," said the counselor.

I continued toward the jetty behind the headland. Then I started to run between the pine trees as I heard cries. Sausage cries. I rounded the headland and saw the jetty and the beach.

Weine and one of his idiots were standing there knee-deep in the water, and between them Sausage was trying to kick himself free. His cries were abruptly cut off when his head was plunged beneath the water.

Weine hadn't seen me. He was too busy trying to drown Sausage. I ran past the last pine tree. This time just words wouldn't be enough against Weine, but I didn't have a sword. It was lying wrapped in my towel. I hadn't been able to smuggle it with me when the counselor was looking at me.

Weine glanced up when I started wading through the water. "Let go of him!"

He let go of Sausage. The other idiot had already let go.

Sausage sounded like he was about to throw up. He tried to get up but fell back into the water.

I raised my fists.

"Don't you have the guts to pick on someone your own size?"

"Stay out of this, Tommy."

"Kenny," I said.

Weine looked like he couldn't make up his mind whether to go for me or Sausage. But Sausage had already started to crawl up toward the shore. The other idiot didn't move.

"And you're two against one," I said, "and you're each bigger than he is."

Weine still didn't move.

"You were really after me, weren't you?" I took a few steps closer. "This is about me, isn't it?"

"He was acting cocky," said Weine. "That's all. He was cocky and he needed to be taught a lesson."

"I'll teach *you* a lesson," I said and took another step.

Weine's flunky looked like he didn't want to be there anymore.

"Tommy! Weine!"

The counselors' shouts echoed high above the lake. You'd have thought Weine and I were on the other side. I caught sight of the sailboat. It must have rounded the headland just as I'd crossed over it. Maybe there was someone on the deck right now watching me through a set of binoculars.

"You get up here this minute!"

"I don't know what we're going to do with you, Tommy."

Matron was sitting behind her writing desk. I had no idea why she even had one. Nobody had ever seen her write anything.

"You pick fights," she continued, "and you won't eat your food."

At supper the oatmeal would be brought out again. It would be colder and the milk bluer or maybe even greener by now, like the bottom of the lake.

"Why aren't you eating?"

Matron got up and from where I was sitting she loomed like a tower. She blocked the sun that had nearly sunk behind the lake by now.

"You can't keep behaving like this."

You can't keep behaving like this, I thought. *We'll just have to wait and see who can keep this up the longest.*

"We're not going to give up," said Matron, seeming to read my thoughts. Though come to think of it, that might not have been all that hard just then. "Don't you go thinking that, Tommy."

"Kenny," I said.

"Right, and then there's all *that* silly childishness."

She sat down again and the rays of sunlight hit me right in the eyes. Matron was like a shadow.

"You're sowing disorder among the others, Tom-m-y."

She drew out the name. *Tom-m-y.* That was what she was like. She wanted to show that she had all the power. Grown-up power.

That was the worst kind.

"Like on the swimming trip. You started fighting."

"I wasn't fighting," I answered, "and I didn't start it."

"The other boy said you did."

"It's a lie."

"You're sitting there trying to tell me that other people are lying?"

"I wasn't fighting," I repeated.

"You went after that boy. Weine."

I didn't answer. It was pointless. It didn't matter what I said. I looked at Matron's thick arms. I didn't want her to grab me again and twist my ear. Or do something worse.

"If this continues we'll have to send you home, Tommy."

She said my name normally now. Only it wasn't my name.

"If this continues, then you'll be sent away."

"What? What do you mean?" I asked because I felt I had to. "If *what* continues?"

"What I've just been talking about! Your refusal to eat.

And the fighting. And all this about accusing us of having stolen a bag of Twist!"

She looked out toward the lake. It seemed she didn't want to look me in the eye. "I'll have you know there are hundreds of children who would love to come out here for the summer."

She looked like she was considering the simplest way to drown hundreds of kids.

"Hundreds," she repeated.

She looked at me again.

"Do you hear me, Tommy?"

I nodded.

"If you don't eat up the good food we give you tonight, we'll have to send you home tomorrow."

"Tomorrow?"

"Tomorrow, right after breakfast," said Matron. Then she smiled. "After the breakfast you don't eat."

Matron looked like she meant it. I didn't know if she could really do that. If there were laws or rules that gave them the right to do that. But I suspected that Matron and the counselors did as they pleased.

"But . . . my mother isn't home," I said.

"There are other camps," said Matron. "If they'll take you, that is."

She stood up.

"So now you know."

"What?" I asked.

"What happens if you don't eat your breakfast tonight, of course."

She smiled a smile that made no one happy. She didn't even look happy herself. I thought about the day-old oatmeal. Matron's head looked like a moon, a black moon, as she looked down at me. Her teeth glinted. She moved her head back and forth as though she wanted to make sure it was firmly attached at the neck.

7

The troop was waiting for me outside the building. Everyone else out front was waiting for supper. I was hungry myself, but I didn't want to think about it. A samurai had to be prepared to endure anything. I needed to have total self-control. I couldn't show any feelings, especially where my stomach was concerned. Everything came from the stomach. A samurai's life force was in his stomach. No one was going to come and tell me what to swallow. It was a question of honor. I could choose to leave all this with the help of the little sword and a single cut to the stomach.

Hundreds of samurai had chosen to leave everything that way. But I wasn't ready to do that. Things hadn't gone that far. Not yet.

"What did Matron say?"

Sausage still looked like a drowned cat. His eyes were red,

his face was blue, and his hair looked like it might never dry. On the march back his teeth had chattered like a rattlesnake.

"Weine and his gang are keeping their distance," said Janne. "They're proving what cowards they are."

"We'll deal with them later," said Lennart and patted his sword.

"Tell us what she said," Sausage repeated.

"They want to send me home," I said.

"They can't do that, can they?"

"They can do anything."

"Then they'll have to send us all home," said Janne.

I looked at Janne. He was in no hurry to be sent off to that farm. He said "home" because he didn't know what else to call it. There wasn't any word that I knew of for a place that was home and yet wasn't.

"I'm not gonna go," I said.

"Hurray!" said Sausage.

"What, so it's been decided?" asked Micke. "They want to send you away?"

"I've been given one last chance."

"What do you mean?"

"The oatmeal."

"Oh shit," said Lennart.

"We can pull the same trick as last time," said Sausage, "and send the dish down to the girls."

"It won't work a second time," I said. "They'll be watching now. And I wouldn't want to do it anyway."

"What did she say—that girl—when she didn't have to eat the liver the last time we passed it down?" asked Sausage.

"Ann. Her name is Ann."

"So what did she say? To the counselor? They didn't make her eat it."

"I don't know."

"Can't you ask her? Maybe she's got a secret. Maybe you could do the same thing."

Sausage didn't know. None of the others in the troop knew. The price for that secret was that there would be girls in the castle. I would have to explain. I didn't want to have to do that right now. I had other things to think about.

"It wouldn't hurt to ask her," said Janne.

"So, can we see the castle?" asked Ann. "You promised that we could see it."

I found her on the branch that reached out over the water. It was the first place I looked. Kerstin was sitting next to her. That was no surprise either.

"There's not much to see," I answered. "It's still only a hut right now."

"Don't even try it," said Kerstin.

"It'll be more fun to see it when it's finished," I said.

"Then you'll have to wait, too, to know what happened in the mess hall," said Ann. She held up her hands and it looked like she was carrying a plate.

"Yeah, I get it."

I looked around. It was completely still. Nobody was spinning on the merry-go-round. Nobody was playing on the swings. Nobody was throwing or kicking a ball around. Everyone was waiting for supper. Many of them were ready to eat anything. The camp's method was to let the children starve and then they'd eat whatever you put in front of them.

"Okay," I said finally, "tomorrow."

"We can see the castle tomorrow?" asked Ann.

"That's what I just said."

"You want to hear what happened in the mess hall with the plate of liver?"

"Tomorrow."

I didn't want to know just then. I wanted to deal with it on my own in the mess hall. I didn't know how, but I wanted to try to handle it by myself.

The sun was still going down. It took hours. It seemed like the sun was also waiting to see what would happen in the mess hall that evening. It was curious so it sent rays everywhere to check up on things.

The mess hall was noisier than usual. I felt dizzy when we went inside and sat down. My ears were buzzing, almost like someone had slapped me.

When the counselor set the plate of oatmeal in front of me, everyone quieted down. She did it before anyone else got their food.

"Eat that up and you can try some of the other good food," she said.

There was a smell of macaroni coming from the kitchen. There might have been sausage too. I looked at Sausage. He was waiting like everyone else. I looked at the plate in front of me even though I didn't want to. It was waiting too. The oatmeal and milk were waiting to work their slimy way down my throat and settle in. Start to grow. Soon rotten oats would be growing out of my mouth. When I thought about it I almost had to throw up. My head was spinning. I closed my eyes and felt them well up with tears. If I opened my eyes now, everyone would see my tears.

I thought about how I'd had a plan, but it was too late. The tears had ruined everything. Someone said something but I didn't hear what. My head was spinning even more. I continued to keep my eyes closed. It felt like I was sitting on the merry-go-round out on the playground and someone was spinning it faster and faster.

Then I fainted.

"Nice trick!"

I wasn't spinning anymore. I opened my eyes and I was lying in my bed in the dormitory. It was Sausage's voice I heard.

He and Janne were sitting on the edge of the bed, but I didn't see any counselors.

"I think you scared them," Sausage continued.

"It wasn't a trick," I said.

"It wasn't?"

"I must have gotten dizzy from not eating for a day," I said.

"It was good anyway."

"Matron came running in," said Janne.

"Did they carry me here?"

"No, you walked by yourself. You don't remember?"

"No."

"You didn't fall off the chair or anything." Sausage wanted to show that it was nothing to worry about. "You just fell forward."

"Where's the oatmeal?" I asked.

I looked around, but it didn't seem to have followed me up to the dorm.

"They took it," said Sausage.

It was still light outside, but the sun had probably seen enough for today.

"I guess they'll be sending me away now," I said.

"I don't think they'd dare," said Janne.

"What do you mean?"

"Children fainting at camp because they're not getting enough to eat? Just imagine if you go and tell someone that."

I nodded.

"Nice trick!" said Sausage.

The shadows had grown longer everywhere. I didn't know how much time had passed. I didn't know what to do. Should I get up or stay in bed? I shut my eyes again. Maybe I should try to get some sleep.

Then I noticed another shadow. I could smell food.

"Tommy?"

I opened my eyes. It was Matron. She was holding a steaming plate in her hand, but I didn't believe it. I thought I was just imagining the plate.

Just then, a memory shot through my mind like a rocket. I was sick and my mother brought me food in bed. The plate was steaming and it smelled good. Maybe it was pork chops. I remembered that my dad liked pork chops. We had pork chops on Saturdays sometimes—every third or fourth Saturday.

I sat up. It smelled of eggs and ham.

"You've got to eat a little, Tommy," said Matron. "Eat this."

"What is it?" I asked thinking it was that same old oatmeal she was holding even though the whole room smelled of eggs and ham.

"Ham and eggs," she said.

The first thing I thought was, *Is it Sunday?* Sunday breakfast in bed.

"I . . . don't want any," I said.

"Don't be silly," she said. "It's fresh out of the pan."

First I thought I'd show off my pride and refuse to accept it. I'd prove that my willpower was stronger than my hunger. Then I thought about how I'd eaten all that other disgusting stuff they'd served before. This didn't seem disgusting at all. And just because it was Matron who was standing here now with ham and eggs, I decided to take it because that proved I had won this round and they had admitted defeat.

I reached out and took the plate. There was a fork lying on it. The plate was still warm as though it had been in the oven.

Matron left the dormitory—a shadow that disappeared. I could hear her footsteps on the stairs.

"Maybe they've been poisoned," I heard from the bed next to mine. "The eggs."

Sausage peeked out from under the blanket. I could see how he had trembled while Matron had been standing there. That was the first time she had ever paid a visit to the dormitory in the middle of the night.

"Matron sprayed arsenic on the yolk."

"Want to try it first?" I asked.

He came over and sat on the edge of my bed.

"Mmm, smells good."

"Want a piece of ham?"

"Nah, you eat it," he said, looking a little worried. Maybe he really believed what he had said about it being poisoned.

I put a piece of egg and a piece of ham in my mouth and chewed. It tasted wonderful.

Then the others began to stir. Micke came over to my bed and then Lennart.

"I wonder what this means," said Lennart.

"Does Matron want to make peace?" asked Micke.

"With me?" I mumbled with my mouth full of food.

"Maybe just for now."

"Never trust a grown-up," said Lennart.

Those were the truest words ever spoken. Never trust a

grown-up. It was impossible to figure out why Matron had done what she had done, and right now I couldn't really think straight. I was starting to feel warm all over my body. When I was really hungry I always felt cold.

"She was scared," said Micke. "They didn't dare let you starve anymore."

"They could have just fried up the oatmeal instead," said Lennart.

"Mmm," said Sausage, taking in the smell again. "If this is what you get out of it, then maybe I should refuse to eat."

"You want those last bits?" I offered, and I pushed the plate toward him. I felt full like I had swallowed a barrel of cement. "It wasn't poisoned."

Sausage gobbled up the piece of egg in half a second. You'd think it was the first time he'd eaten a fried egg.

"Mmm!"

"So what happens now?" asked Lennart.

"What do you mean?" I asked, and I stretched out my leg, which had started to cramp from balancing the plate on it.

"Does this mean peace?" asked Lennart.

"I certainly hope not," said Micke.

"Nothing's changed," I said, "except that we won this round."

"Maybe they'll send you away anyway?"

"It's a lot of work for them," I said. "They're too lazy to organize everything they'd need to get me out of here."

I pointed at the plate that Sausage was busy licking.

"That was easier."

"So what happens the next time we refuse to eat?"

"We?" I threw my legs over the edge of the bed and stood up. "Did anyone other than me refuse to eat?"

"The next time someone refuses," said Micke. "You or one of us."

"They'll get ham and eggs!" said Sausage.

"I'm not so sure about that," I said.

The counselor stared at me for a long time when she set down the plate of oatmeal in front of me at breakfast. It was a freshly cooked portion. I wasn't hungry, but I ate it. It wasn't the right moment for another refusal. I didn't see Matron, but I knew she was waiting in the wings. Maybe she was planning her next move. Just like me.

After breakfast I gathered the troop.

"You go on ahead," I said.

"What for?" asked Sausage.

"Micke, you're in command," I said without answering.

The troop had just disappeared into the forest when Ann

and Kerstin came up. It was a close call.

"Guess you don't want to know the secret anymore," said Ann.

I knew what she meant.

"I want to know it," I said.

"You did all right without it."

"I want to know what you said, Ann."

She looked at Kerstin. I thought I saw Kerstin smile.

"It's all about keeping your eyes open," Ann continued. "Especially at night."

"Yeah?"

"One night a few weeks ago I heard something outside. It was almost morning and I was already awake. I went over to the window." Ann pointed across the playing field. "You can see the counselors' barracks from there."

"I know," I said.

"But you don't know what I saw!"

"No."

"I saw one of the counselors standing outside the door to the barracks hugging and kissing a man!"

I didn't say anything. I understood. If Matron heard about it, the counselor would be fired on the spot.

"What did they do then?" I asked.

"Then he left."

"Uh-huh."

"It was nearly morning, like I said."

"And you reminded the counselor about that in the mess hall?"

"Yes, but I didn't say anything. I didn't have to say anything. I was the only one who saw her that night, and she saw me. She looked up and saw me in the window."

Ann looked at Kerstin.

"So I didn't have to say anything to her when I walked over with the dish."

I thought I saw Kerstin smile again. "I almost didn't think you were going to start eating," she said.

She had seen me when I ate my oatmeal.

"You think I gave in?"

"No, no."

"You die if you don't eat," said Ann.

"Or get sent away," said Kerstin.

"I got something else, too," I said, and I told them about my Sunday breakfast at night.

"You could have refused," said Kerstin.

"You think I should have?"

"No," she said after a short pause. "Then they would have sent you home."

"What difference would that have made?" I asked without looking at her.

"There'd be no one to show us the castle," she answered.

"Are we ever going to get to see this castle?" asked Ann. "Or did you just make it up?"

"You haven't told the others yet, have you?" Kerstin looked at me. "You don't dare, do you?"

"Aren't you the leader?" said Ann. "Aren't you the one in charge?"

"You don't understand."

"What don't I understand?" said Ann and smiled. "Japanese?"

Kerstin didn't smile. She realized this was not something to joke about.

"*Sei-i tai shogun*," I said.

"What's that?" asked Ann.

"It's Japanese."

"What does it mean?"

"Great general who fights barbarians."

"And that would be you?" asked Ann. She looked at my sword implying that she didn't think it was worthy of a general. "Are you the great general?"

"Come on; let's go," said Kerstin. She had started to look worried. She understood. "Let's just forget about this for now, Ann."

"What?" said Ann. "I'm just curious. Who are the barbarians, Kenny?"

I didn't answer.

"Are they the ones who serve you ham and eggs in bed?"

"Stop it!" Kerstin said loudly.

A few of the kids in the courtyard looked up.

Ann turned around and walked off.

"Sorry," said Kerstin.

"You didn't say anything."

"Yeah, but she was with me."

"Forget it."

"Guess I'll never get to see the castle now."

"I haven't even seen it myself." I tried to smile. "Like I said, it's not finished."

"What are you going to do with it? When it's finished?"

"Live in it, of course."

"What about all this?" she said, and she waved toward the camp, the playground, the grounds around it, the beach, the trees at the edge of the forest, the buildings, the gate to freedom, the kids themselves, the guards, Matron, everything.

"We won't need all this," I answered. "None of this is going to be here anymore."

"What do you mean?"

"It's just a feeling I have," I said.

The forest always felt like a very big place. It went on forever all the way around the world. This forest was connected to other forests throughout the country, and they continued across all the borders into other countries. This forest was the same forest all the way up to the far northern end of the country, and on into Finland, and then Russia, Siberia, Mongolia, and China. All the way to the sea and up onto the other side of the sea, to the Japanese island of Kyushu. That was the biggest of Japan's southern islands. There was a forest there. I had seen pictures. I wanted to walk in that forest. I wanted to do it before I grew up.

"How come you know so much about Japan?" asked Kerstin.

She walked next to me in the forest. We were far away from the castle at the other end. I still didn't know how I would be able to show her the castle. But I was the leader. I wasn't a *shogun*, but I was a *daimyo*. I had the highest rank, and I could do as I pleased. Whatever I thought was best for us. Anyone in the troop who didn't like it could leave.

"I can read," I said in answer to her question, "and look at pictures."

"Have you got a lot of books about Japan?" she asked.

"I don't have any, but there are libraries."

"Why Japan?"

"It's not really Japan. It's more the samurai."

"But they lived in Japan, right?"

"Sure."

"Are there any left?"

"Sure."

"You never hear about them," she said.

"The samurai prefer it that way," I said.

"How can you become a samurai?" she asked. "You're not even Japanese."

"I'm trying to learn," I said.

"To become Japanese?" Kerstin smiled.

"That, too," I said.

"Why don't you go to Japan then?" she asked.

"Good question," I said.

"I was only joking."

"It's no joke. I'm going there."

She almost looked like she believed me.

"But what's so exciting about the samurai?" she continued.

"It's better than this," I answered.

"This? What do you mean by 'this'?"

"This. What we've got right now," I said. "Not just the camp but . . . all of this." I opened my arms wide to include the forest as part of what I meant. "This . . . life or whatever you want to call it."

"Life? Your life?"

"Yeah . . ."

"You want to escape from what you have, you mean?"

I didn't answer.

"It's just some kind of dream you've got," she said. "You can't just dream about being a samurai."

"It's not a dream," I said. "You'll see it's not a dream."

A samurai was something you were born to; it wasn't something you were appointed to. Your parents had to be samurai, otherwise you weren't a proper samurai. But you could sometimes be adopted by a samurai family—if you were worthy of that kind of honor.

That was in Japan. But this was Sweden. Actually, the province where I was living was called Småland. It was in the south of the country, just like Kyushu was in the south of Japan. Småland had sort of been its own kingdom a long time ago. That was because there are lots of mountains and forests here, and that made it difficult for other warlords to attack and plunder. That's how it was in Japan as well. The terrain on most of the Japanese islands was mountainous and covered in forest, and it was difficult to travel from one area to the next. You couldn't rule Japan like a single country. Each part of the country, especially the four biggest islands, had their own warlord.

I didn't think I'd get adopted in Japan. But I could live like a samurai in Småland and learn everything the samurai knew. Not just this summer. Always.

I had walked in a circle through the forest with Kerstin, and we had come back to the camp. We hadn't been gone very long. I would have liked it to have taken a little longer.

"Now you have to go back to your troop," she said. "And some day, maybe you'll have the courage to take me to the castle."

"I'll go back when I feel like it," I said.

"To show them that you're in charge?"

She smiled again. I nearly smiled back.

We were standing just inside the gate. One of the counselors came out of the main building and walked straight up to us.

"Matron wants to speak to you, Tommy."

"Again?" asked Kerstin.

The counselor didn't answer. She just peered down at Kerstin.

"You come with me," she said. She tried to take my hand, but I pulled it away and put it on my sword.

We walked across the playground. The little kids were shouting on the swings and the merry-go-round. One of them had gotten hurt and the cries floated up toward the blue sky. There were no clouds up there today either. I hadn't heard any weather report for some time. You didn't need to this summer. It was like some country far away where the sun was always shining.

The counselor shut the door behind her when she left. Matron had pulled down the roller blinds in her office. It was dark but I could see well enough. I could see her sitting there behind her desk. She was framed by the roller blinds behind her. Like a painting.

"So, do we have a deal, Tommy?" she asked.

"Kenny," I answered. "My name's Kenny."

"Did it taste good? The food last night?" she asked and stood up.

I nodded.

"I hope you're grateful, Tom—Kenny," she said as she walked around the desk. "We could have sent you away."

I nodded again. I'd heard that before.

"If you're good to me, then I can be good to you," she said standing in front of me. "We shouldn't have to fight each other, you and I, Kenny."

She stood just inches from me. It seemed like the room had turned pitch black. I suddenly felt very afraid—more afraid than ever before. It felt like anything at all could happen here inside Matron's office.

"We know each other, after all," she said, and she put her hand on my shoulder. "You're a big boy now, Kenny. You could help me out here at the camp."

"H-how?" I asked.

"You could set a good example. Show the other kids. Show them how to behave."

That's exactly what I'm doing, I thought to myself.

I tried to think away the fear. To swallow it. I tried to make myself feel tough.

Matron came even closer.

"We have to cooperate," she continued. "Otherwise it'll be chaos out there." She kept her hand on my shoulder. It felt like a sledgehammer. "And we don't want that do we? Chaos?"

Sure, I thought. *That's just what we want.*

She took her hand away quickly and stood straight up again.

"By the way, I've got something that I think belongs to you."

She turned around and took out a brown paper bag from the desk, opened it, and pulled out my bag of Twist.

8

The bag of Twist lay on the table between me and Matron. It was see-through and looked unopened, but there was no way of knowing for sure. I could see the small, colorfully wrapped chocolates inside. My mouth watered, but I didn't want to let her see that. I hoped it wouldn't show if I spoke. But I wasn't so stupid as to not realize that it could have been a different bag of Twist altogether. Matron could have bought it especially for this interrogation.

"It was a mistake," she said, nodding at the bag. "It somehow ended up in a drawer we thought was empty."

Empty. Whoever put the bag of Twist in the drawer must have seen that it wasn't empty anymore since the bag of Twist ended up there.

Matron held out her hand and poked at the bag as if I hadn't yet noticed it was there.

"So you were right, Kenny."

Really. So what did she want me to do now? Tell her that I forgave her and the counselors and the cook and the whole camp? That I forgave Weine? That I forgave my mom and my dad, and the whole country and the whole world?

"You can take it," she said.

I heard what she said, but I guess I must have looked like I hadn't. My jaw was probably still hanging open in surprise.

"You can take your bag of Twist," she repeated. "You can take it with you."

My god! Nothing like this had ever happened before. It ought to be big international news. A guy at a summer prison camp with a whole bag of Twist! A whole bag!

But I knew that the bag was just bait. Or a bribe. Matron wanted to make a pact with me. This wasn't for free. It had to be paid for twice over, or three times, or more.

"So we're friends then?"

I nodded. That was the smartest thing I could do at this point.

"We'll help each other out?"

I nodded again. I didn't know how she could help me or how I could help her, but it didn't matter right now.

"Take your candy now," she said. She smiled like she had just done the most charitable deed and the greatest coup of the summer all at the same time.

The warriors had continued building the inner stone wall while I had been gone. It needed a lot of stone. The three walls around Himeji Castle, which was built in 1609, for example, covered an area of one hundred thousand square yards.

Our walls wouldn't be that big, but they'd be big enough. We were building without any mortar just like in Japan. It was much better that way because then each stone could move a little without causing cracks in the entire structure.

Fluttering above the wall was the standard with our coat of arms. It was a black circle against a white background. Two black lines that were the same thickness as the circle passed through it. We were going to make a few smaller banners— long thin ones. The smaller ones were called *nobori* and were meant to be carried when the big battle came. A large samurai army had several dozen standard bearers. It was dangerous to be a standard bearer since they always had to stay close to the commanders, and that's where the battle was the fiercest. Your banner was always worn on your back. We were going to sew a banner holder on the back of our armor. Once we'd finished making our armor. Once we'd gotten the breastplates, side plates, and back plates mounted. We were trying to get hold of some cardboard to make the plates or preferably some plywood. A good suit of armor could save a samurai's life.

I hid the bag of Twist underneath one of the cornerstones of the inner stone wall. No one had seen the bag. I had hidden it underneath my shirt and sword strap. I had to think about it more before I told the others about my meeting with Matron. I didn't know what to do with the bag. As I walked through the forest I regretted that I had accepted it. But at the same time I didn't have any choice.

"You were gone a long time," said Micke.

"You've made good progress on the wall," I answered.

"What were you doing?"

"Nothing."

"Nothing? For almost two hours?"

Sausage and Janne entered the glade carrying a couple of big rocks. They dropped them next to the wall, which was a yard high in some places.

"We weren't supposed to have any secrets," said Micke.

"What secrets are you talking about?" asked Sausage, who'd come over to us.

"Nothing."

"You looked strange when you came back," said Micke.

Sausage, Janne, and Micke all looked at me. Did I look strange? I felt strange. I had a secret that I didn't know what to do with. I didn't want to carry it around with me.

"Matron called me into her office."

"Are they going to send you away?" Now it was Sausage

who looked strange—almost like he might start crying. "They can't do that."

"The opposite. She wanted to make a pact."

"Between us and her?" asked Micke.

"Well . . . between me and her."

"I don't understand," said Janne.

So I told them.

"It's gotta be some kind of trick," said Micke.

"She said nothing about the castle?" asked Janne.

"I'm not sure she knows about it."

"Of course she does," said Micke. "She knows everything."

"She's a witch." Sausage looked at me. "But what are we going to do with the bag of Twist?"

"What does anyone do with a bag of Twist?" said Micke, grinning.

"It feels like we're playing right into her hands if we open it," I said.

"You've already accepted it," said Micke.

"It was yours from the beginning," said Sausage.

"You didn't do anything wrong," said Janne.

"They're the ones who've done wrong," said Sausage. "You could have reported them to the police for stealing."

We ought to report them to the police for worse than that, but it wouldn't do any good. The police had come over to my house a few times when things had gotten rough at home after Papa had drunk too much, but having the police come hadn't helped Mama for more than a short time. Then it got even worse.

"When we're finished with the wall, we'll eat the whole bag," I said. "Then we'll celebrate."

Really, we ought to wait to celebrate until the whole castle was finished. But I had a feeling that the chocolate would be all dried up by then.

Janne and I found a wall that was already built in a glade when we went looking for small rocks. The glade was about half a mile from the castle.

This one was more than a yard high all around. It was the foundation of a cabin that didn't exist anymore. When you saw the foundation you could imagine the rest of it. Strange that we hadn't seen that glade before—like it hadn't been there. But you had to make your way through thick forest to get there. It was like a dry jungle. There were no paths. Whoever lived there must have made paths walking back and forth, but it was all overgrown now.

"We could have built our castle here instead," said Janne.

"It's too far away."

Janne looked off toward the forest. It was thinner on the other side; you could see a field between a few pine trees. Then we heard a train whistle.

"This is closer to town," he said. "Closer to town than the camp."

"Want to go?" I asked. "Into town?"

"You mean . . . now? Or this summer?"

I didn't know what I meant. It was just something that popped into my head. Maybe it was because Janne would soon be leaving this community and province altogether and be sent to a farm somewhere far away.

"I don't know," he said, and turned to me. "Do you?"

"Why not?" I asked.

I didn't know why I said that last bit either. Sneaking off into town was a definite one-way ticket out of here. It had never been done. Maybe I'd also end up on some farm, at least until Mama got back from that rest home. She was back at that place again. They called it a rest home, but I knew what it was, of course. I knew what an asylum was. Maybe it was going to be her home now. Maybe I had nowhere to go anymore, unless I wanted to spend the rest of my life in the nut house.

"Maybe we can wait," he said.

"Another time," I said.

"But it's a good idea."

"We can leave in the morning and be back in time for supper," I said.

"Tomorrow?"

"Why not?"

In the afternoon the troop was forced to play burnball again. Not that I complained, but we had other things to do.

This time Kerstin had ended up on the other team. When she ran past me the first time, on the way to third base, she threw up a hand and laughed as if she thought something was funny or that she and I had an amusing secret.

I was glad when she rushed past me and did that. I felt warmer for some reason even though the sun was already shining.

Then we switched. When it was my turn at bat, I saw that she stood farther back than all the others. If I were smart I would just bunt the ball off to the side so no one would be able to catch it before it hit the ground, or else I'd really belt it out over the lake even though that wouldn't count. But at the same time, I wanted Kerstin to catch my ball in midair. I wanted to hit it higher and farther than ever, but I also wanted her to catch it in the air.

I connected. I could feel it throughout my body when I hit it right. The impact sort of throbbed through the bat and my arm and shoulders and head. The ball went super high and then super far, and I had to put my hand over my eyes to see when it started to come down in the harsh light.

I saw Kerstin standing completely still like a statue with her hands cupped toward the sky like she was praying or something. She didn't have to move an inch. The ball was on its way straight toward her.

I knew that I had gotten a perfect hit—a lot more perfect than anyone here realized since the ball followed the exact trajectory I had planned. I kept my hand over my eyes to protect them against the sun. I saw Kerstin stay where she was while the ball descended lower and lower until finally she caught it before it reached the ground. I wanted to shout out and cheer, even though we weren't on the same team.

"Aren't you going to run, Kenny?"

It was Sausage. He was next up at bat.

I took off while the ball was slowly on its way back. It rolled into the grass and stopped. Someone else picked it up and threw it a little farther, and on it went. When I passed Kerstin, she laughed again that same way, and I put up my hand to wave at her. Then I slammed into the ground face first. Just like that, *wham!* I felt how my nose got scraped and my face went all warm, but it was a different kind of warmth than I'd felt before. This felt like fire.

"Can't you even stand on your own two feet?"

I heard the voice next to my ear, but it sounded like it was in a tunnel. My head was spinning.

"If you can't even stand, then you shouldn't run!"

I recognized the voice now. I blinked and tried to get up. I felt a burning in my nose again and I could see drops of blood falling onto the ground. I saw feet and legs and grass. I felt a thickness in my throat and I gagged and spat and there was blood in my spit.

Weine said something else, but I didn't hear what it was. It must have been his legs that I saw right in front of me.

I was just going to let those legs have it when I felt someone lifting me up.

"Oh, dear," said the counselor.

"He tripped on that root," I heard Weine say.

"This looks pretty nasty," said the counselor.

It sounded like Weine was laughing under his breath.

"We'd better take a look at that nose," said the counselor. "You'd better come with me, Tommy."

The spinning subsided, but I still had a little trouble seeing. Maybe I had a concussion. Maybe my nose was broken. The counselor held me by the arm, but I tried to pull free. I could walk on my own. I didn't expect anyone to tell on Weine, but someone must have seen him.

"I think he needs a stretcher," I heard Weine say.

I didn't like Weine's voice. I blinked again and now I could see him. He was smiling. I didn't like that smile. Standing right behind him was Micke, and he was smiling, too, maybe not realizing that I was looking.

9

It felt like a whole army had marched over my nose, but no bones seemed to be broken. If I had looked in the mirror, I probably wouldn't have recognized myself, but I had no intention of looking in any mirrors. I never looked in mirrors. Why would I do that? I looked the way I looked.

The samurai used mirrors to capture everything in the world just as it was. The mirror was holy in the sense that it didn't lie. What you saw in the mirror was the true image of your surroundings. You might not recognize it, but that was how things really looked. The mirror was handed down from samurai to samurai just like the sword. But no samurai looked at himself in the mirror. They held it up and used it to catch the sun. And everything under the sun.

Like me. And Kerstin. She was blocking the sun, and I

was happy about that. It hurt my nose even more when the rays of sunlight hit it with a sizzle.

I sat up in the bed where they had laid me. I hadn't asked to lie down there. The counselor had left the room. The window was open and I heard the burnball game continuing. Someone hit the ball. It sounded like a hard and long hit. I hoped it wasn't Weine. Or Micke. I remembered how Micke had looked. He'd had the smile of a traitor and the eyes of a weasel. You could have held up a mirror in front of him and asked, "Who is this? Friend or foe?"

"It doesn't look too bad," said Kerstin.

"What doesn't?"

"The weather," she said and let out a laugh. It sounded like pearls of glass bouncing on the floor.

"Nothing's broken," I said and felt my nose. I had virtually no sensation in the tip of my nose.

"No ambulance then," she said.

"I'm not going to give him the satisfaction."

"Who?"

"Weine," I said. "Did you see him trip me up?"

"Maybe he didn't mean to."

"Didn't mean to!" My nose began to sting like it had gotten angry, too, when Kerstin said that. "Of course he meant to. It's obvious. As obvious as the sun rising in the morning."

Someone turned the door handle. The counselor was

back. The room was starting to become cramped. I wanted to get out of here.

"You just take it easy, Tommy." She picked up a couple of bloody cotton balls from the floor. "No more burnball for you today."

"My name's Kenny," I said, and I slid down from the bed until I was standing on the floor. In a few years I wouldn't need to slide down. My feet would already be on the floor when I was sitting on a bed. In Japan the beds were on the floor. It didn't matter if you were a kid or a grown-up. Everyone sat on mats on the floor and ate from low tables.

The sun burned my nose as we stood on the steps. Everyone else was at the front of the building. I heard the sound of the burnball game again.

"Didn't they want to know why you left the game?" I asked.

"I told them I had a stomachache."

"Do you?"

She didn't answer. A gull flying over the lake started laughing as though it had just heard a joke.

"You don't have to keep me company," I said.

"When are you going to show me the castle?" she answered.

I heard shouts and hits coming from the burnball field again. It sounded like a war.

"We can go this way," I said, and I pointed toward the forest on the other side of the beach. We could follow the edge of the lake for a bit and then take a left into the forest and reach the castle from the other direction.

There was a smell in this part of the forest that I didn't recognize. It was like a different forest. The trees looked different. Maybe it was because you could glimpse the lake through the trees like a reflection from a mirror. It was darker here than in the other forest.

"What's that smell?"

"I don't smell anything." Kerstin looked around. "I guess it's just the forest."

"There's something else."

She looked around again. Almost everything was shrouded in half-darkness despite the reflections from the lake—or because of them.

"Must be gloom then," she said.

"The gloom?" I saw how it covered the path we were walking along.

It seemed to move with us. "Gloom doesn't smell, does it?"

"When it gets darker, it smells different," she said.

"Have you noticed that it smells different at night? When the sun goes down?"

"Yeah."

"There are other smells that come out then."

"Yeah. And other colors."

There were already other colors on this path. Shadow colors.

"And in the end no colors at all," she said.

"Black," I said. "The black's still there."

"That's not a color," she said.

"What is it then?"

"It's a . . . nothing. I don't like black. It's what you wear to funerals. And I don't like funerals."

"Who does?" I asked.

"I don't know what the point is of having them."

"Well . . . I guess the dead sort of have to be sent away somewhere."

"Sent away?"

"You can't exactly have them sitting at the kitchen table at home, can you?" I pictured my dad sitting in front of me with a cup of coffee. Or a glass of whiskey. "Or in front of the TV."

"Maybe they have a favorite show," said Kerstin.

Now we were in the other part of the forest—my forest. The shadows lifted and disappeared among the branches. It got lighter and it smelled lighter too.

"What do you think a dead guy's favorite TV show would be?" Kerstin continued.

"Could be anything," I said. "It's all crap anyway."

"How do you know? Do you watch them all?"

"Not a single one."

"But you still know that it's all crap?"

I didn't know anything, but I didn't want to talk about that right now. We didn't have a TV at home. A lot of people had started buying TVs when they first came out a few years ago, but Papa had said that it was just a bunch of crap, and then . . . well, then we couldn't afford one.

"I thought you had seen some samurai movies on TV," said Kerstin.

"Do they show movies like that?"

"I don't know. But I guess they should. They show Ivanhoe and William Tell. And Robin Hood."

"They're not samurai," I said. "They're from England."

"William Tell's from Switzerland."

"Well, they're not from Japan anyway," I said.

"How far away is Japan?"

I looked down at the path.

"All you have to do is start digging and eventually you'll get there."

Like at a funeral, I thought as soon as I'd said it. Kerstin looked like she was thinking the same thing, but she didn't say anything.

Funerals were also meant to make people remember. Everyone had to remember for as long as possible. I hadn't liked it when I'd been forced to sit in church with Mama and her sisters and all the others. I didn't want to go to any more funerals. I didn't want to remember that way. I wanted to remember in my own way without having to follow all those rules. I didn't like graves, either, or cemeteries. You were supposed to stand in front of a gravestone and remember, but it was just a stone. It had no soul. It was an unnecessary weight lying on top of the one buried below.

The glade opened up. The shadows were all gone now. We were there.

"It's not finished yet," I said.

"You already told me that."

She walked toward the wall. Somehow, it seemed lower than it was. It was the same with the towers. I looked at them through different eyes now. They had become unfamiliar— like they had been built by others.

"It's nice," she said.

"It could be one day," I said.

She looked around. I thought the whole area looked smaller now. I shouldn't have shown her the glade and the castle with its courtyards and walls. I didn't feel proud of the castle anymore.

"It's really nice," she said and smiled.

"You think so?"

"Sure."

"There's a lot left to do," I said.

"I can help you." She held up her hands. "Many hands—"

"Spoil the broth," I said. But I immediately regretted having said that.

"That's not how it goes," she said and smiled again. She didn't seem to take offense. "And you'll need help here if you're going to be finished this summer."

"We won't be finished this summer."

"But you've got to, don't you?"

"We'll continue," I said.

"Continue? After the summer?"

I nodded.

"I don't understand," said Kerstin.

It wasn't something I could explain, exactly. I didn't even understand it myself. Not yet.

The burnball tournament was still underway when we got back to the camp. The shadows along the path were longer. There was a smell coming off the lake. Mud and reeds and murky water. They were screaming louder than ever at the burnball field.

There was a man standing by the thick branch that reached out over the water. On the grass in front of him was a black box. I knew what it was. So did Kerstin.

"Uh-oh," she said. "I forgot about that."

"Me too."

The man was there for the summer photo. We were all supposed to gather beneath the tree, everyone was supposed to look happy, and then the man would press a button at the end of a wire.

In last year's photo I stood behind the tree. Just when the man shouted, "Cheese!" I hid.

I had stood in approximately the same spot where the man was standing now. When everyone was looking at him and he was looking at everyone through the camera, I had slipped behind the tree. But I was still in that photo.

He saw us coming. It was the same man as last summer wearing the same hot blazer.

"Well, it's that time again," he said. "Isn't this fun?"

"What's fun about it?" I said.

"Getting your picture taken, of course." He laughed as though the idea that it might *not* be fun was really hilarious. "Don't you like photos, kid?"

"Not of me."

"A good-looking kid like you," he said and winked. "Of course you should have your picture taken." He nodded at Kerstin. "And your girlfriend too."

"She's not my girlfriend," I said quickly.

"Oh she isn't, huh?" he asked and laughed again.

"He's not my boyfriend," said Kerstin.

"I see," said the man. "So you just happened to bump into each other, eh?"

He winked again like he had gotten a speck in his eye or had a nervous tick. Maybe photography made you nervous.

Mama took me to a photographer once when I was two, I think. I don't remember it, but he must have tricked me into laughing because I was laughing in the picture. I was sitting in a wicker chair. There was a curtain hanging behind me. There were no colors—just black and white.

A few years later it was time again, but then I didn't laugh. I remember that I was there and that the photographer told me to laugh but I didn't want to. Papa was supposed to have come along to the photographer's, but we couldn't find him when we were about to leave.

At home there was a photograph of Mama and Papa standing in some square and laughing into the camera. That was before I came into the world. Maybe that was why they still looked happy. Maybe if I hadn't been born, they would be as happy now as they were then, standing in that square laughing and baring their white teeth like they were in a toothpaste ad. I was there too. I was in my mother's stomach, which was sticking straight out.

It was summer in that picture—eternal summer. The

picture was black and white. It wasn't big, but it had a thin silver frame that made everything look even more black and white. For as long as I could remember, the photo had always been standing on the chest of drawers in Mama and Papa's bedroom, but when Papa died, Mama moved everything out to the living room, including the chest of drawers. I used to see her standing there looking at that photo for ages as if she were trying to remember something that she'd forgotten.

As if she were looking for something in the photo.

The mailman's motorcycle sounded like a jet rumbling through the forest when Kerstin and I walked back to the camp. The rumbling lingered like the sound of the jet that Janne and I had seen.

I had received a letter. It was from Mama, of course. I had been thinking about not writing to her anymore so I wouldn't get any more of her letters, but at the same time, I wanted them. I didn't want to read them and I did want to read them. It wasn't actually the words I wanted to read; it was more the fact that something made it into the camp from outside. That there was another world out there. The mailman on his Triumph boneshaker was proof of that. A Triumph Bonneville. He had brought something for me. Just the envelope would have been enough.

I sat on the steps. The courtyard was silent. Everyone was mostly just sitting in the shade waiting for the sun to set. It was a strange summer. The sun had almost become an enemy. Your whole head started to hurt if you stood in the sun in the middle of the day, and there were fire warnings everywhere.

On the radio they had talked about forest fires up north. A few days ago two transport planes had flown over us with huge sacks of water. I had followed the planes with my eyes but I couldn't see when they dropped the water. It must have been like a waterfall. But the fire hadn't been put out.

"Is the fire going to come here?" Sausage had asked when he stood next to me as the planes were flying over us.

"It depends on which way the wind's blowing, I guess," I had said. "If it's blowing from the south, you just don't know."

"What'll happen then?" Sausage had asked.

"The whole camp will burn up," I had answered.

"Don't you say burn *down*?"

"First it burns up and then it burns down."

"What does?"

"The whole damn thing. The camp. Everything."

"How about the castle?"

"We'll save that."

"We don't even have a moat with water in it," Sausage had said.

"The fire's not gonna come from the forest."

"What do you mean?"

I didn't actually know what I meant. It was just something I felt—or thought. That there was a fire that was coming. Like a dream while you're awake.

The letter from Mama was shorter than usual. There were smudges on the paper; or maybe she had been eating supper while she was writing and spilled something she was drinking. Some of the letters were fuzzy. An *F* could look like a *B*.

But I could still understand what she'd written.

She was going to be away when I came home after the summer. She would explain when she got back.

I was supposed to go stay with a friend of my mother's who was not *my* friend. She had a boy who was three years younger than me who wasn't my friend either. They lived about half a mile from us on a really boring street where there were no shops.

Everything's been taken care of, wrote Mama. *You don't need to worry. Everything's going to be fine.*

Not the way you think, I said to myself, and I crumpled up the letter and stuffed it into my pocket.

"Is it bad news?"

Lennart had sat down next to me on the steps.

"My mom," I answered.

"Bad news, then."

"I can't go home," I said.

"What do you mean?"

"Nobody's going to be there in the fall, so I can't go home."

"Well, that isn't good news."

"Just like Janne," I said and nodded toward Janne.

He was standing in the middle of the playground throwing a ball against the wooden fence—*boink-boink-boink-boink-boink.*

"But he's going to a foster home."

"It makes no difference."

"What are you gonna do then?"

"I'm not gonna go where they want me to go!"

"You're not?"

"I'm gonna show them."

"What are you gonna show them?" asked Lennart.

"What I can do. Where I can go."

"And where's that?"

"It's a secret. For now."

Micke wanted to speak to me behind the woodshed, where there hadn't been any wood for a long time. There was still an ax in the chopping stump. Some grown-up with the strength of five men had buried it in the stump last summer. I had tried to pull it out but hadn't succeeded.

"Are you all right?" asked Micke.

"Sure, thanks to you and your help."

"What do you mean?"

"What happened to Weine? Huh? What did you do to him?"

Micke looked around to see if someone was listening to us, but most of the kids were standing outside the mess hall waiting for supper.

"We had to consult with you first," said Micke. "We couldn't just go after him." He looked around again. "Or the others. He's not alone, you know."

"Maybe there are more of them than there are of us," I said. "Or will be soon. Before long they might outnumber us."

"It doesn't matter. We're stronger."

Now he looked like someone you could rely on. I became unsure again. I hadn't liked that smile, but maybe he had just gotten nervous when Weine tripped me.

"If it comes down to a fight, we're stronger," said Micke.

"They're not the ones we should be fighting," I said.

"Who is, then?"

A counselor opened the main doors to the mess hall.

Everyone poured in. I could hear another counselor shouting inside. The windows were open and her shouts were carried off across the lake.

"Sit STILL! Be QUIET! Stop all that RACKET!"

I nodded toward the mess hall. It was an answer to Micke's question.

"Soon they'll come out looking for us," he said.

"I wonder what's for supper," I said.

"I wonder what's for dessert," said Micke.

I laughed.

10

Matron seemed twice as big as usual. The counselors had dragged me off to her office since I had refused to eat my supper. It wasn't something I had planned on doing, but when the plate was standing there in front of me, I couldn't even get myself to lift the spoon.

Matron wasn't alone.

"You've met Christian, haven't you?"

She nodded at her son like it was the first time he'd been there, but he came every summer. Maybe he was going to take over after Matron.

"I don't know what to do with you anymore, Tommy."

Christian didn't say anything. He seemed twice as big as Matron. He was a giant who filled most of the room. That made me think of the ax that was buried in the chopping stump in the woodshed. It must have been Christian who planted it in the stump. It would have taken incredible strength. A frightening strength.

She turned to him.

"What should we do with him, Christian?"

"What's he done?" Christian smiled. He was getting a kick out of learning about all the terrible things I had done. He looked like a film star. His golden-yellow hair was thick and wavy, combed into an Elvis-style pompadour, and his teeth were big and white when he smiled. He wore a white shirt tucked into a pair of jeans that looked like they'd come straight from America. He himself looked like he'd come straight from America. There was a silver chain hanging from his neck and he was tanned in a way that made his teeth look even whiter and his hair even more like gold.

"He picks fights," said Matron. "He doesn't eat. He tells lies. He incites the other children against us."

"This little shrimp?" Christian took a few steps forward. I flinched.

"See that? He's afraid of his own shadow."

"He's pretty cocky out there, I can tell you," said Matron. "He thinks he can do as he pleases when no one's watching."

"Feeling cocky now?" asked Christian. He took another step and grabbed hold of my arm like I was a fly and he could pull my wing off with one little tug. "Think you can do as you please, huh?"

He let go of my arm and grabbed my sword as though *it* was my arm—which it was, of course; it was just an extension of my arm—and he yanked the sword from my belt.

"What's this, huh?" He held up my sword. It looked like a matchstick in his hand. "What kind of crap is this?"

"That's his sword," said Matron and laughed. "He's always got it with him. Says he's a samurai."

"Sam . . . samurai? What's that? Some kind of Chinese crap, huh?" Christian looked down at me. "Are you Chinese, kid? What did you do, get lost? Dig in the wrong direction?"

He laughed just like Matron. They laughed together. Then he looked at her and held up the sword again.

"You let them go around with things like this? He could poke somebody's eye out."

"You might be right," she said.

"Of course I'm right," he replied, and he grabbed the sword with both hands and snapped it in two.

I saw how the wheels were turning in Sausage's head. Something had happened that couldn't happen. Sausage and I were the only ones in the dorm. We were confined indefinitely. Sausage had been punished for causing a fuss when they dragged me from the mess hall.

"You're the only one who knows," I said to Sausage.

He didn't really seem to understand it yet. He was trying to work out how a sword could be broken in two.

"You realize you can't tell anyone about this?"

He nodded.

"That's good, Sausage."

"What are we going to do now?" he asked after a while.

"Make a new one," I said. "Make a new sword."

"But . . . you had that one for a long time."

"A samurai can lose his sword in different ways," I said. "I haven't lost my honor. Not when it happened like that."

"I guess."

"You could say that I've already got a sword, even though I don't actually have one. You see what I mean, Sausage?"

"I . . . think so."

"I've always got a long sword with me—in my mind," I said as I looked at the short one, my *wakizashi*, that I'd taken out of its hiding place under the floorboard. "In my mind's eye, I've always got it with me, and tomorrow I'm going to make it real so that I can hold it in my hands."

"Are they going to let you?" asked Sausage.

"They can't keep me locked up all summer."

"What's going to happen with the castle?"

"We'll keep building it, of course," I said.

Sausage looked like he wasn't convinced.

"Nothing can keep me in here," I continued.

144

"What if they send you home?"

"They can't. There's no one at home. You know that."

Sausage didn't say anything more. We looked at the short sword. I carefully thumbed the edge of the blade. It was sharp.

Christian and Matron had made a big mistake when they didn't look for this sword and destroy it too. They didn't know what a samurai used it for. They would be surprised when they understood.

Sometime during the night I had a dream that was full of fire. I was standing in the middle of the flames and I saw no one else. I heard someone calling out, but I didn't know who it was. Then I stood outside the fire and saw the flames rise all the way up to the sky. Only there was no sky, just fire. I was on my way back into the fire when I woke up covered in sweat. It was like I had really been in there in my dream. I still had the smell of smoke in my nostrils.

Everything was quiet. Then I heard a scraping noise outside. It sounded like someone was moving around on the playground. Then it went silent again. And then that scraping noise again. The window was like a panel of light on the wall. As I walked over to it, the floor felt cold beneath my feet. Sausage was rocking back and forth in his sleep as though he were trying to escape his own dream. Everyone in the dorm room was asleep. There were hours still to go until morning.

I lifted the blinds and looked down onto the grounds. I didn't see anything except the grass that was more gray than green in the moonlight. Everything was grayer down there. All the colors seemed to have turned over in their sleep. I heard that scraping sound again and I realized what it was. I recognized the squeak of the merry-go-round. It was on the other side of the building, but the sound circled around and around the building too. It creaked again, a hollow scraping sound from the rusty metal.

Someone was sitting on the merry-go-round in the middle of the night slowly spinning around. It was a drawn-out sound that was barely audible. It wasn't something that would wake you up.

I went back to my bed and sat down and thought. It didn't take more than a few seconds. I pulled on my shirt and shorts but left my sandals underneath the bed. I strapped on my short sword. The blade felt cold against my leg.

When I sneaked down the stairs, the moon was shining into the mess hall, splitting it into two parts. One for the kids who behaved and one for the kids who didn't.

As I stood on the stairs, I heard the creak and the scraping sound again from the turning of the merry-go-round. Whoever was sitting on it must be pushing off every so often with their foot. I continued silently down the stairs and then snuck outside.

The grass was wet beneath my feet as I headed cautiously around the corner. Even though the days were so hot, the nights were still wet. Or maybe that was why it was wet. It may have been moisture from the lake rather than rain. The nights had already started to get a little longer and there was more and more moisture. The summer would soon be over—and not just for me.

I could see the lake from where I stood at the corner of the building. The fog floated above the surface of the water and headed in toward land. I could see the merry-go-round. It was spinning very slowly, but enough that you could hear it. Someone was sitting on it. Someone who was just a shadow moving around and around. When the merry-go-round swung toward me I saw the surging glow of a cigarette in the face of the person sitting there. It was Christian.

I took a step back, but he didn't see me. I don't think he did anyway. His face was turned toward the main building. There was something over there that was holding his interest the whole time. I looked too. All I could see were the windows to the girls' dormitories.

All of a sudden he put his foot down and the merry-go-round came to a stop with a little creak. The glow of his cigarette surged again, lighting up his face. It looked like a mask. He glanced toward the lake before he headed off in the other direction and disappeared behind the corner of the building. Then I heard a car engine start up. I ran to the other side and saw the red tail lights disappear through the front gate. Where was he going? It was still nighttime. He had a room here at the camp.

It hit me that Christian must have been here as a child. Matron had been the camp overseer for many years, and when Christian was little, he must have been here. How had it been for him? Had he been allowed to play with the camp children? Had he been alone out in the forest? I tried to picture him as a child among the others, but I couldn't see him—not any more than I could see him now that the lights of his car had disappeared.

I didn't see Christian the next morning, either, when I sat in Matron's office. She wasn't looking at me but was looking through the window like she was keeping an eye out for him too. Then she turned to me.

"We can't find your mother."

"She's not home," I answered.

"We know that." Matron looked out the window again, this time as if she were looking for my mother. "But she doesn't seem to be at the . . . other establishment either, the rest home."

The *es-tab-lish-ment*. As if our home was an establishment, too, and the rest home was the other one. Like a castle. Only there was no castle in town. The castle was here.

"So we haven't gotten hold of your mother." She turned away from the window again. "Do you know anything, Tommy? About where she might be?"

I thought about the letter I'd gotten from Mama, the last one where the letters were a little smudged. She had written that she'd be away when I came home and that she'd explain when she got back. *Everything's been taken care of*, she had written. *You don't need to worry. Everything's going to be fine.*

I shook my head.

"You must know something."

I shook my head again.

"Kenny?"

So, it was Kenny now. She really wanted to know.

Then I started to worry. I hadn't understood until now.

"What's happened to my mother?" I asked.

"Nothing's happened. Not that we know of. We just wanted to speak to her, but she wasn't there."

"What about?" I asked.

"What?"

"What were you going to talk to her about?"

"You, of course. About your behavior here."

I nodded.

"You do understand that, don't you? You realize that you've been behaving badly?"

I didn't answer. That wasn't what I nodded about.

"We can't keep you here. You do realize that, don't you?"

She looked out the window again. I couldn't see out, but I knew the sun was shining and the sky was blue. It was just as hot as last week and the week before that. There was going to be another swimming trek around the lake today too. I knew that the children were being lined up outside the building right now.

"That's what we were going to talk to your mother about."

Matron ran her hand over her hair that was put up with pins at the back of her neck. They were like secret weapons. "But now we don't know what to do with you."

I almost felt happy that Mama wasn't there to answer when they called. She had chosen the right moment to leave.

"The people at the rest home have to report it to the police," said Matron. "She's been missing for over twenty-four hours."

The rest home. I saw Mama's face in front of me but it was smudged like the letters in her note.

"Didn't you receive a letter?"

My thoughts were interrupted. Matron looked down at me.

"You got a letter the other day, didn't you?" she asked.

I nodded. There was no lying about that.

"Wasn't it from your mother?"

"Yes."

"What did she write?"

"Nothing."

"Where is it?"

"It's . . . gone."

"Gone? What happened to it?"

"I dropped it in the forest."

"I've never heard the like. You dropped a letter in the forest?"

I nodded again. She looked at me like she knew very well I was lying, but she couldn't force me to say where I'd hidden the letter. In that sense, she knew me. And I knew her.

"What did she write?" asked Matron again.

"Nothing special. Except that she was gonna be gone when I got back."

"That's nothing special? What are you saying? I've really never heard anything like it. Where was she going?"

"I don't know."

"And where were you supposed to go while she was away?"

Of course I wasn't going to tell her that. I wasn't going to let Matron send me to Mama's friend and her stupid kid.

"She was going to take care of it," I said.

"Take care of it? How?"

"She was going to let me know."

"My God," said Matron. "What a family."

She got up. I got up, too, as a reflex.

"You can go join the others," she said.

As I was on my way out the door, she called to me.

"Don't think you're off the hook," she said from her desk. "As soon as we get hold of your mother, you're out of here."

One day passed and then a second. I gathered that an alert had been sent out for Mama, but that they hadn't found her yet and that was why I was still at the camp. I wasn't under house arrest anymore and could move around freely like before. I thought some police officer would come and question me about Mama but nobody came.

I was sitting behind the wall of the castle's inner courtyard with the letter from Mama in front of me. The paper had gotten all crumpled and thin. It was about to fall apart into shreds. It looked old like parchment or something. The letters looked different—almost like they were from some other language.

Everything's been taken care of. You don't need to worry. What did she mean by that? What had been taken care of? Why didn't I need to worry? Because it *had* been taken care of? Because it *would* be fine?

I was worried, but she had written to me. She would write again when she got to wherever she was going. She'd be there soon. And why should she have to tell the people at that place where she was going? They couldn't tell her what to do. Nobody could tell Mama what to do, and no one could tell me what to do either, not even Mama.

I heard the troop practicing with their swords outside the moat. Maybe it was Sausage's new sword I heard. It was almost bigger than he was—like Musashi's oar when he defeated Kojiro.

My own *bokken* lay next to me. It wouldn't be easy even for Christian to break that in two.

I hadn't seen him since he'd sat there spinning around on the merry-go-round in the middle of the night. He'd had a strange glint in his eyes when he'd looked at me in Matron's office. It was something I hadn't really picked up on last summer. Maybe it was more noticeable now that he'd grown up. Something frightening. I hadn't been able to see how he'd looked when he was staring up at the girls' window, and I was glad about that. He had driven off, and when I sat there in the castle, I hoped that he would disappear too.

11

I closed my eyes and the shouts from the sword practice seemed to be echoing in a dream. It was my dream. One day we would wake up once this summer was over. Would the ruins of the castle still be there, like the remnants of a dream? Something we knew we had experienced but couldn't remember in detail?

I opened my eyes and saw the stones that made up the wall. They would still be there for others who came after us, but that wasn't good enough for me. This was my dream and my castle.

"Wanna go into town? Have you got the guts?"

I had closed my eyes again and his voice was like a loudspeaker in my ear.

Janne was bent over me. He was still wearing his shoulder, knee, hand, and neck guards after the practice session. He looked like an ice hockey player. The only things missing were the skates. Even his helmet looked like an ice hockey helmet.

He was rubbing his shoulder.

"Are you hurt?"

"Micke really laid into me."

"He always does."

"This was worse than ever," said Janne. "It was like he was angry about something."

"He's always angry."

"So are you."

"Am I?"

"Yes."

"Aw, get out of here."

"The question was whether we should go into town," said Janne.

"You mean right now?"

"We'll make it back for supper."

"What supper?" I asked and Janne laughed.

"Okay," I said. "We've got nothing to lose."

The field overlooking the town was like an ocean as far as you could see. The wheat swayed in the wind like waves. We tried to stick to the edge of it so the farmer wouldn't see us and come racing over in his tractor accusing us of destroying his crop. It had happened before.

"You could have a really big battle here," said Janne. "The two biggest samurai armies in the land."

"It's a good spot," I said.

"Our troop versus Weine's," said Janne.

"Weine's aren't samurai."

"But we could fight them just the same."

"The farmer wouldn't like it."

Janne looked around and then turned to me.

"Do you know what I think?" he asked.

I shook my head.

"Before this summer's over, we're going to have to face them in a big battle. A real battle. A serious one."

"Not only them," I said.

"What do you mean by that?"

"We have other enemies."

"The counselors? Matron?"

"Them as well."

"Who else?"

"We'll see," I said. "But I can feel it."

"Feel what?"

"I'm not sure yet."

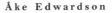

A hitchhiker was standing at the town line. He was on his way out at the same time that we were on our way in. His backpack was on the ground in front of him. As we passed him on the other side of the road, he raised his thumb at us like he was wishing us good luck.

"Do you think he'll get a ride?" asked Janne.

"We'll see if he's still there when we go back," I said.

"Wanna bet on it? I'll bet you ten that he'll still be there."

"Okay," I said, although I didn't have any money. But I was sure he'd get a ride before we left town. He seemed pretty confident. He had a cap and sunglasses and looked pretty cool. Maybe too cool, in fact. Anyone ready to offer him a ride might want to see his eyes first.

Then he took off his sunglasses and squinted at us.

"He's Japanese!" I said.

Janne took a good look at him over his shoulder.

"Nah, he's just squinting." He kept on walking.

The Japanese hitchhiker put his sunglasses back on. Did he just want to show me what he was? I wanted to cross the road and ask him, but I didn't have the nerve. He would probably think I was an idiot.

"If he is Japanese, he might not get a ride," said Janne

turning around to look again. "He'll still be there when we go back."

In that case I would lose money, but it would be worth it. I knew there were people from foreign countries who hitchhiked their way around Sweden. I saw someone from Africa once. That was from a train as we were passing through another town. He looked pretty glum, that African, as if he knew he'd never get a ride. But I'd never seen a real live Japanese man before.

We continued walking toward the town center. It wasn't a big town, but it was bigger than the one I lived in. There was a bridge over a wide river and a park on the other side. The park had a hot dog stand at one end, so we went over there and asked if they had any burnt hot dogs they wanted to get rid of.

"We throw them away," said the lady behind the counter. She had to lean out of the window in order to see us. "It's not good for you to eat burnt food."

"Don't you have any that are just a little burnt?" asked Janne.

The lady laughed, drew her head back inside, and started doing something behind the counter. Then she handed over two hot dogs in buns with mustard. There didn't seem to be any burnt bits on either hot dog. They were brown and juicy.

"Here you go, boys," she said.

"How much are they?" I asked.

"They're on the house!"

She reached out a bit farther with the hot dogs. The front of the stand started to smell like paradise. She smiled. I'd been there before, but I didn't recognize her. She looked nice. She should have had the job of cook at the camp.

"You look hungry, boys. Don't they give you any supper at home?"

We tried to answer but we couldn't. We were drooling at the thought of what was to come. Besides, we didn't really have a home. But we each had a hot dog. We carried our delicious supper into the park and sat down on a bench.

"There are actually some nice grown-ups," said Janne before biting into the end of the hot dog sticking out of his bun.

I nodded and took a bite of my own. It was the best thing I'd tasted all summer. We chewed away as we watched a couple of guys about our age paddling down the river in a canoe. One of them had a fur hat with two feathers sticking out of it. The other had a bow and some arrows hanging down behind his back. They looked like explorers I'd seen once in a book about Lewis and Clark. The one with the hat raised his hand toward us in some kind of greeting. I raised the hand that wasn't holding the hot dog. A samurai with a hot dog. The canoe vanished underneath the bridge and emerged on the other side. The river flowed into the lake where the summer camp was. I'd seen a canoe on the lake last summer. Maybe it was this one.

"Why don't they have a canoe at the camp?" wondered Janne. "I like canoes."

"They probably think we'd use it to get away," I said.

"We get away anyway," said Janne.

"But it's easier if you have a canoe. All you need to do is jump in from the dock back home."

"*Back home?*"

"What do you mean?"

"You said 'back home,'" said Janne, "like the camp was our home."

"A slip of the tongue."

"Really?"

Was it really a slip of the tongue? Right now the camp was actually the only home either of us had. My mother was on the run and Janne was going to be sent to a foster home.

"Jump in from the dock in the moat," I said. "That's home, isn't it?"

Janne laughed.

"We'd better fill it with water then," he said.

"Have you heard the one about the loons who spent day after day diving into a swimming pool? One day somebody came along and asked if they were having fun, and they said yes, they were, but it would be a lot more fun tomorrow because they'd be filling the pool with water."

"Ha ha," said Janne. "Have you heard the one about the loons who left the asylum every morning and came back every evening with bruises and broken arms and legs?"

"How'd they leave the asylum if their legs were broken?"

"Do you want to hear the joke or not?" he asked as he stuffed the last of his hot dog into his mouth and swallowed it almost without chewing.

I nodded.

"Okay. One morning one of the nurses followed them and saw how they climbed up one of the tallest trees in the forest. Then they hung from the branches and shouted, 'I'm ripe now,' let go, and fell to the ground."

"Ha ha," I said.

"They were pretending to be windfall fruit, get it?" asked Janne.

"Yeah, I get it."

"Have you heard the one about . . ." he began but stopped when the canoe came gliding back into view and the explorer in the front saluted us once again.

"Maybe they want something," said Janne.

"Maybe they want to fight," I said. "We're trespassing on their territory."

The two explorers brought the canoe to a standstill in

the middle of the river. Then they turned in a semicircle and paddled toward us, heading for the narrow strip of sand between two pine trees. They stepped into the water and beached the canoe on dry land. The one with the hat said something to the other one; then they stood motionless between the two trees. They were about twenty-five yards away.

Janne put his hand on his sword.

"Take it easy," I said.

"Guess they could be peaceful," said Janne, taking his hand away.

"Maybe they don't think we are," I said. "Here they come."

Janne prepared himself for battle, but he didn't draw his sword. If he had, he'd have been forced to kill one of the explorers before we could go back to camp.

The explorers stopped several feet in front of us. The archer was holding his bow in his hand, but his arrows were still in his quiver. The one with the hat was holding a tomahawk. It looked heavy.

"Who are you?" he asked with a local accent.

"Samurai." I remained motionless. "We're samurai."

"Are there any more of you?" He looked at his companion and then back at me. "How many of you are there?"

"Just us two."

Janne stepped forward.

"We come in peace," he said.

The archer muttered something I couldn't make out.

"Where are you from?" asked the other one. He was swinging his tomahawk back and forth as if he were weighing it. It must have weighed a pound. If that landed in your skull you'd find yourself in the happy hunting grounds pretty quick. "You're not from around here, are you? I've never seen you before."

I told him where I came from.

"Anyone who comes from there is an idiot," said the archer. "That place is a real sewer."

Almost everyone there is an idiot, I thought. He was nearly right.

"You're a long way from home," he said. "Did you catch a ride here? Or did you run away?"

"We walked here," said Janne.

They looked surprised. The city I was from was almost thirty miles away.

"You walked all the way here dressed like that?" said the one with the hat as he eyed us up and down.

"We've come from the summer camp," I said.

"You mean you've run away?" asked the archer. "Uh-oh."

"Have you been there?"

"No, but we've heard about it. There are one or two kids from around here who were forced to spend time there."

"Who?"

"Uh . . ." He looked at the boy with the hat. "Didn't Benke get sent there?"

"Isn't he there now?"

The archer turned to me.

"Do you know Benke?"

"What does he look like?"

The archer described him. It wasn't anybody I recognized.

"Come to think of it, they've moved away," said the one with the hat. "His old man got a job up north, I think."

"Who are you?" I asked.

"Explorers," said the boy with the hat. "What did you think?"

I pointed to the canoe.

"Mohawks maybe?"

"You don't know much about Indians, Mr. Samurai."

"Can you paddle all the way to the lake from here?" I asked.

There was a water system from the town to the lake that was shorter than the route we took through the field. Janne and I sat in the middle of the canoe. The explorer with the hat sat in front of us. The feathers on his hat were taken from a rooster. They were so big that they could even have come from an eagle. His hat was triangular and looked pitch black in the shade. He was wearing long shorts, and his fringed leather jacket lay in the bow of the canoe, some of the fringes touching the water like fingers. His back was so tanned that it also looked black as night, and the muscles rippled between his shoulders as he paddled. I wouldn't have liked to face him in a wrestling match. With swords that was something else. But he only had his hunting knife stuck into his belt at the back. It looked like a real Bowie knife, though. I recognized the handle from pictures in books at the library back home. The library seemed very far away right now, like it was on another planet or even in another solar system.

I looked around at the archer, who was paddling behind me and Janne. He looked back, but he didn't smile or anything, and I could see in his eyes that he knew we were heading into a storm—into big trouble. He was wearing a fringed, belted jacket, and the big buckle over his stomach looked like gold when the sun burst out from behind the trees on the hill we were passing. The quiver was slung over his shoulder, and the bow lay at his feet ready to be picked up in just a second. I could see it was made of juniper, which is the best wood for bows. It looked strong and fast and ready to send his arrows anywhere he wanted them to fly.

The archer was wearing some kind of suede pants that looked like they'd been walking all over the world almost by themselves, and he wore Indian moccasins on his feet. The one with the hat wore suede boots of a kind I'd never seen before—worn and brown like a second skin. It looked like these guys had everything—like they'd done some real exploring in America and bought everything they needed when they were over there. The archer had a fur cap tucked in his belt. A telescope that looked a hundred years old lay in the back of the canoe. When we'd jumped into the canoe earlier in town, they'd even told me it was built on the designs of canoes originally made by the Mohawk tribe. Maybe they were just putting me on, but I wanted to believe it. It felt safer to believe it.

There were some perch lying in the bottom of the canoe, but I couldn't see a fishing rod. They must have used their bare hands to control the line. The life of an explorer didn't seem too bad. They didn't have to go to bed in a dormitory every night. My guess was that they slept under the stars. They looked wild. Maybe they'd forgotten that they ever had a mother or a father. That got me thinking about Mama again. I didn't want to give the impression of being worried. Not even to myself. So I said to myself: *Kenny, everything's just like always. You'll go back home at the end of the summer and your mother will be standing in the doorway and she'll try to hug you, but then she'll have to hurry back into the kitchen to make sure the pork chops don't get burnt.*

Maybe some news about Mama had arrived by now. That would make them start looking for me and find out that I'd run away. I hoped the news would come after we'd made it back to the camp.

The river started getting wider, which meant it would soon be flowing into the lake. The trees were thick on both sides. It was like a jungle. The sun shone down on the water making it look like it was covered in a layer of gold. Water runners were jumping around on the gold. You could see millions of insects buzzing in the sun's haze. We swallowed lots of them every time we breathed, so we were pretty well fed.

That was why I never felt hungry, even though I didn't eat the food served up at the camp. But I sure was hungry when the lady in the hot dog stall gave us the hot dogs. And to be honest, I felt hungry again as I looked at the perch and thought about what they would taste like once they were skewered on a branch and grilled over a campfire.

I turned around. Janne smiled. His face was as tanned as mine, but I could see that his chest was white behind his samurai armor. He looked puny compared to the archer paddling behind him. The archer's arms were thick like he'd spent all his life paddling. Maybe he had. Maybe he was born in this canoe. The one with the hat might have been born in it too, although they didn't look like brothers—no more than Janne and I did. We hadn't asked them their names, and they hadn't asked us either.

I faced forward again, but I was still thinking about Janne. He was used to not having a mom or a dad. Was that something you could get used to? It must be worse having a stepmother and stepfather. I'd never heard of a nice stepfather, but of course, everybody at the camp exaggerated. I preferred not to think about the possibility that I might have to have stepparents.

"This is how it ought to be all the time," I heard Janne saying behind me.

"We could get ourselves a canoe too," I said.

"Wouldn't that be expensive?"

"Ask them," I said.

"We got ours from my dad," said the archer.

So he had a dad.

I thought about our castle. That was our canoe and our river and our jungle.

The summer camp looked small from the middle of the lake, which made it seem like a nice place. I'd been out in the camp's lifeboat but not this far out.

"Have you been here before?" I asked.

"Lots of times," said the one with the hat.

"I've seen you."

"Did you recognize us in town?"

"No, but I've seen the canoe."

"Have you ever gone ashore?" asked Janne. "By the camp?"

"It seems much too dangerous," said the archer.

I turned around and saw that he was smiling. But he wasn't kidding.

"The counselors probably would have beaten you to death," said Janne.

"Yes, and served us up as the evening meal," said the one with the hat.

"Kenny doesn't eat the food at the camp," said Janne nodding in my direction.

"Pleased to hear it," said the archer.

"'The missionary was a good man,' said the cannibal," the one with the hat joked.

"What did the cannibal say when he didn't like the food they served on the airplane?" asked the archer.

Janne and I shook our heads.

"'I'd like something tasty! Bring me the passenger list!'"

We laughed. I don't think they could hear us back at the camp. I couldn't see a soul on the playground. Maybe they were all searching for us in the woods. In that case I hoped our troop had camouflaged the castle.

"How come you go there, anyway?" asked the archer, as he waved his paddle toward the headland where the camp sat. The outline of the buildings now looked sharper, as if the sun had switched on an extra searchlight when he asked.

"Because it's fun," said Janne.

The explorers knew he didn't mean that. You only needed to look at the buildings.

"We've heard stories about it," said the one with the hat.

"What kind of stories?"

"That they beat you, for instance."

"That's no big deal," said Janne.

"They stole my bag of Twist," I said.

"You're kidding," said the archer.

"And then they made me take it back again."

"I don't understand," said the one with the hat.

So I told him.

12

You should all run away," said the archer, starting to paddle toward one of the headlands to the east where we could land without being seen from the camp. "Or report them to the police or something."

"Do you think they'd believe us?" asked Janne. "We can't prove anything. Can you go to the cops if you don't have solid proof?"

"Well . . ."

"What about your parents?" The boy with the hat had turned around to face us.

Janne and I looked at each other. We didn't answer. The one with the hat seemed to understand. He didn't ask any more questions but faced forward again and continued paddling.

When we reached shallow water, Janne and I climbed

out of the canoe. We could hear voices and shouts from the camp. Maybe they were playing burnball again.

"Let us know if you need any help," said the archer.

"How would we get in touch if we did?" asked Janne.

"Smoke signals," said the one with the hat.

"It might be too late by then," I said. I imagined smoke, thick black smoke, rising up over the camp and the lake and the fields, spreading as far away as the town.

"Too late for what?" wondered Janne, but I didn't answer.

The castle was deserted. The only sound was a magpie shrieking high up in the trees. It sounded like a warning cry.

The clearing was not far from the headland where the explorers had dropped us off. I was still thinking about those perch as I walked to the castle.

"They've done quite a lot," said Janne looking around.

The walls were a little higher. So was one of the towers. But the moat was just as dry as before. The only thing that could fill it would be a cloudburst.

"The castle will be ready to move into soon," I said.

"You mean we're going to move in for real?"

"It's almost time."

Somebody had made a fire in front of the castle. You could tell it had been a small fire so the smoke wouldn't be seen from the camp. I poked at the embers. Some of them were still glowing. It was dangerous to leave glowing embers in the forest, especially when the summer was as hot as this one.

"Did they leave the fire burning?" asked Janne.

"Maybe something happened."

"Here?"

He looked around. Everything looked normal. The only thing that was new was the magpie chattering. I looked up but I couldn't see it.

"There doesn't seem to have been a battle, anyway."

"Maybe something happened somewhere else," I said.

"At the camp?"

We listened in that direction, but we knew it was too far away to hear anything, not even if they'd had a hundred Triumph motorbikes revving their engines on the playground.

"You mean that something lured the troop away?"

"Let's find out," I said as I kicked soil over the embers that had started to cool down.

Even though we were getting close to the camp, we still couldn't hear anything. The sun was going down, but it wasn't time for supper yet. We couldn't see anybody in the woods near the big entrance gates. Everything seemed to be just as deserted as the castle had been.

"Something must have happened," said Janne.

The merry-go-round on the playground was spinning without anybody on it. I noticed that the wind had picked up, and when I looked up I could see clouds in the sky above the lake. There were black lines like mourning bands around the edges of the clouds. There was a rumble of distant thunder and several black clouds came rolling in. It all happened in the space of a few minutes. Clouds were scudding across the sky now.

"All hell's going to break loose," said Janne.

"Has everybody gone inside to take shelter from the storm?" I wondered.

"They couldn't have known about it until five minutes ago."

Suddenly a figure came rushing out of the woodshed. As he ran toward us, the first raindrops began to fall. The air had thickened. It felt like a woolen sweater. There was already a smell that made you think you were on the other side of the world in a jungle. The boy running toward us had short legs that started to gleam as the rain poured down.

It was Sausage.

"Where have you been?" he shouted through the rain.

We didn't have time to answer. There was a flash of lightning over the lake. It was followed just a few seconds later by a loud crash all around us. Then we saw another flash bigger than the first one. After a couple of seconds there was a huge explosion in the sky.

"It's dangerous standing out here!" yelled Janne.

We ran toward the woodshed that Sausage had just come from.

There were others standing inside. It was the troop.

"What are you doing here?" I asked.

"It's raining," said Mats.

"But you were in here before it started, weren't you? The playground was completely deserted when we got here, and the thunder and lightning hadn't started yet."

There was another crash. The rain was pouring down like Niagara Falls. A whole summer's worth of rain was falling all at once. The shallow trough around the merry-go-round was already filling up with water.

Our moat would get filled up now. This would be the last stage. After this cloudburst, the castle would be finished. As long as the roof on the tower held up under the rain, we'd be able to move in.

"Why were you hiding in here?" I asked again.

"We weren't hiding," said Mats. "We were waiting."

"Waiting? Waiting for what?"

"For the others to head off in the other direction."

"The search party," said Sven-Åke.

"Search party? For us?"

"No. They haven't noticed you're missing yet."

"Who is missing then?" I asked.

I had a strange feeling that I already knew what Sven-Åke was going to say.

"Kerstin," said Lennart—who hadn't spoken until now—repeating the name I expected.

"Kerstin?" repeated Janne.

The others looked at me. I realized they must know more than I thought. Maybe they knew that I'd shown her the castle. Everybody must have seen us talking to each other.

"Did she run away?" I asked.

"Nobody knows."

"What about her friend? Ann?"

"She's out looking too," said Sven-Åke.

"And why aren't you?" I asked.

"We . . . might know where she is," said Lennart.

They hadn't wanted to tell Matron or the counselors.

Nor Christian.

"He's come back?" I asked.

"Yesterday evening," said Lennart, "or during the night."

"I saw him last night," said Sven-Åke, "under the window."

"Which window?" I asked.

"Ours, of course," said Sven-Åke. He meant the window nearest his bed in the dormitory, which was opposite mine and directly above Kerstin's. "He was sitting on the merry-go-round smoking. I thought I heard something squeaking, so I looked out and there he was with a red glow coming from his mouth. It was like he was spying on us. I was scared he would see me."

"Are you sure it was your window he was looking at?" I asked.

"What do you mean?"

"The girls," I said. "I'll bet he was staring at *their* windows."

"I don't understand," said Sausage.

"Lucky for you," I said.

"Hmm," mumbled Sausage, who was maybe starting to catch on after all.

"You didn't want to say anything to the grown-ups about Kerstin?" I said.

"There's something weird about him," said Lennart. "About Christian."

"Does it have something to do with Kerstin?"

"I'm not sure."

"You said you might know where she is," I continued. "So, where is she?"

"In the woods, but in the other direction."

He pointed.

"How do you know?"

"We saw her. Sausage saw her."

"She was running like a deer," said Sausage.

"When was that?"

"A few hours ago. This morning."

"Why didn't you run after her?"

"I didn't know she was running away," said Sausage. "All I saw was that she was running. I mean, everybody runs around here, Kenny." He looked at the others. "But when they started saying she'd disappeared, I realized . . ."

I thought about Kerstin when he said that. No doubt she could run like a deer—or like a pony with her mane of hair flowing behind her.

"Did she look scared when she was running?" I asked.

Sausage shrugged.

"But you knew enough not to say anything to the grown-ups?"

I felt a cold chill at the back of my neck as I said that. My hair felt like it wanted to stand on end—like I was having a nightmare or had just had one and still hadn't woken up properly. What had happened while Janne and I were in town?

"They looked . . . strange," said Lennart. "Both Matron and Christian."

"How? When?"

"When they told us to go out and search for her. I don't

know . . . Matron came out of her office and Christian was in there, and then he came out too, and both of them looked . . . well, strange."

"Strange?" I asked. "What do you mean *strange?*"

"As if they . . . *knew.*" Lennart looked at the others. "Isn't that strange? But they looked like they knew somehow."

"Knew? Knew what?"

"Why Kerstin had run away, of course. And that she *had* run away."

"She probably ran away for the same reason as the rest of us," said Sven-Åke. "None of us wants to be here."

"I don't know," said Lennart. "Matron looked sort of . . . shaken."

"Let's go look for Kerstin now," I said.

It stopped raining just as quickly as it had started. Clouds were still racing across the sky, but now they were heading off to another country. There were big, black pools of water all over the playground and courtyard, but they would soon evaporate. Water surrounded the merry-go-round like a moat. It had never occurred to me before that the rut had become so deep from all the kids kicking at the ground over the years to make the merry-go-round spin. It could be a hundred years old, that moat.

The forest looked like a different place now. It was darker, wetter.

"She was running in that direction," said Sausage pointing into the darkness.

The sun had disappeared behind the tops of the fir trees on the other side of the lake. We could have used a flashlight. The fir trees seemed to be leaning over us. When I looked up, the sky was no more than a little hole. A black bird fluttered past like a dragon overhead.

We moved farther into the trees. The bird let out a cry as though warning somebody. To our right I could see the lake glittering like silver. Steam was rising from it like it was a hot spring. I'd almost forgotten what it was like after a heavy rain. The ground underfoot was wet and warm. Steam was rising from there too. I noticed that I was sweating so much that it was getting hard to see. Everything was blurred. I wiped my eyes with my hand but everything went blurry again before I had time to blink. It was like trying to wipe water from your face when you were swimming right down at the bottom.

"She could have run for miles," said Janne.

"Then she'd have to get around the lake," said Lennart.

I could see the lake glint again in the darkness. It seemed to be trying to tell us something, to show us something. Was it something to do with Kerstin? I felt that cold chill at the back of my neck again.

"Can she swim?" asked Janne, seeming to read my thoughts.

"Like a fish," said Lennart. "I mean, she won the swimming competition a few weeks ago, didn't she?"

"Did she try to swim across the lake?" asked Sausage.

"Let's go down there," I said, although I didn't want to. The lake felt like a more dangerous place than the forest right now. It had turned black. All the silver had vanished from the surface.

We made our way through the dense undergrowth. Lennart was in front of me, and I wasn't quick enough to get out of the way when he let go of a branch that hit me in the face. It hurt, but I had more important things to think about.

The water's edge was overgrown with reeds. I took a step out and immediately sank down into the water.

"Your face is bleeding," said Sausage.

"What?"

"You look like you've got war paint on."

"We don't use war paint," I said, and I thought about the explorers. The archer had two red stripes over his cheeks. No doubt I looked a bit like him now.

"I can see something moving out there," said Janne.

We continued wading through the reeds. It was still shallow at this point, but soon the bottom would become muddy and we'd be forced to turn back. The mud in this lake was like quicksand. If you got caught in it, you couldn't get out.

"It's a boat," said Sausage.

The reeds were thinning out. The mist over the water was starting to fade. I could see something long and narrow moving slowly over the surface.

"It's a canoe!" said Janne. "The explorers! They're still here!"

As the canoe drew closer to the shore, I could see that the two explorers were not alone in the canoe. We pulled it in through the clumps of reeds and there sat Kerstin shivering and shuddering after swimming with her clothes on. Her lips were the same dark blue as the sky.

"All of a sudden, there she was swimming," said the archer.

"In the middle of the lake," said the one with the hat. "We almost ran right into her in the mist."

"Kerstin," I asked gently, "are you all right?"

She was sitting in the middle of the canoe. Her soaking-wet T-shirt was hanging off her, looking like it weighed a ton.

"She hasn't said a word," said the archer. "We didn't really know what to do until we saw you."

"But we realized that we shouldn't take her to the camp," said the one with the hat.

"Did you see anybody?" I asked.

"No. The place looks deserted. But it wasn't easy to see anything in this mist."

Kerstin stood up and stumbled out of the canoe. She lost her balance and I grabbed hold of her arm. She was freezing cold—colder than you usually are after a swim.

"Why did you run into the lake like that?" I asked.

"I . . . heard something and thought that he . . . that they were after me."

"Who's they?"

She didn't answer.

"You said *he*. Do you mean Christian?"

She nodded.

"What did he do?"

"He . . . he . . ." She couldn't bring herself to say any more. Instead, she started shivering twice as much as before.

"She could catch pneumonia," said Sausage.

"We've got to get her some dry clothes," said Janne.

"She's got her stuff back at the camp," said Sausage.

"NO!" screamed Kerstin.

She looked at me and then at the others.

"I don't want to go there!"

"There's nobody there," said Janne. "Everybody's out searching. For you."

"But . . . somebody always stays behind," said Kerstin.

"Put this on for now," said Janne, starting to take off his shirt.

"We've got an old blanket in the canoe," said the archer. "She didn't want to put it around her out there."

"Okay," I said and started walking toward the camp. "Wait here."

"Where are you going?" asked Sausage.

"I'm going to check the camp."

Everything was quiet as I walked across the playground. Most of the water had already drained away from the trough around the merry-go-round, leaving a layer of mud behind. The fog over the lake was gone. A canoe wouldn't be able to hide out there anymore. Nor would a swimmer.

It looked like everybody was still in the forest searching. I thought I could hear some shouts, but it might have been birdcalls.

I knew which dorm Kerstin slept in but not which bed. But I did know that she kept her suitcase underneath her bed and that her name was stenciled on the side of it.

As I snuck along one of the walls in the mess hall, I could hear an awful clattering coming from the kitchen. Maybe the cook was busy killing a beaver for dinner.

It was quiet in the girls' dormitory. All the beds were made in a way that would have won first prize in our dorm.

Kerstin's bed was the third on the right. I could see the case underneath it, but it was too big for me to carry back to the canoe.

I almost felt like a burglar when I opened the case, but I had to do it. I took out some sweaters and underwear and a pair of jeans and some socks. There was a pair of sandals at the bottom and I took those too.

Then it occurred to me that I didn't have anything to carry all the stuff in. I tried one of the cupboards; there was a pile of sheets inside just like in our dorm. I took one of them, put Kerstin's things on it, tied it into a bundle, and was just about to slip out through the door when I heard a voice I didn't want to hear.

"Didn't you find her?"

I stayed in the girls' dormitory. Somebody muttered something a ways off, and I realized that Matron was talking through the mess hall window.

"She's got to be close by," I heard Matron say.

Somebody mumbled something again.

"She can't have gotten *that* far," said Matron. "She's got to be close by."

More mumbling.

"How should I know?"

Mumbling again. I thought it sounded like one of the counselors.

"Let's just deal with one thing at a time," said Matron. "We can take care of them later."

Them. Take care of *them.* I guessed that she was talking about us. Me.

I didn't know if somebody had stumbled across the castle while they were out searching, or if they would have cared even if they had found it. They wouldn't have known what it was anyway.

I looked around the dorm. The window farthest away from me was half open. I could see the courtyard, the playground, the merry-go-round, and beyond that, the lake.

I tiptoed across the floor, unhooked the window, and opened it slowly so that it didn't squeak like the merry-go-round usually did. I couldn't see anyone when I leaned out to take a look.

It was only about six feet down to the ground, so I dropped the bundle of clothes. It landed on the grass with a slight thud that nobody could have heard. I jumped out, landed next to the bundle, and ran toward the trees without looking around.

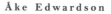

The path became dark when we moved in among the biggest fir trees. It was a roundabout route we were forced to take so as not to bump into all the people out searching. But they wouldn't keep going for much longer.

"Pretty soon they'll call the police," said Sausage.

"I don't think they will," I said. "Not tonight, at least."

"Why not?"

I didn't answer and neither did Kerstin. She was in front of me and behind Janne. After me came the archer followed by the one with the hat. They had pulled the canoe in among the trees and camouflaged it with twigs and branches. It was impossible to see it if you didn't know it was there.

"Maybe we can be of some use," the archer had said when they came along with us.

They were tough explorers who always had to be ready for anything. Maybe they could smell the scent of an approaching battle.

Kerstin had gone behind the canoe to get changed. When she came back, her face wasn't quite as white as it had been, and her lips were not so blue.

She still hadn't said what had happened.

It was quiet in the woods as we approached the castle from the north.

It struck me that I hadn't seen Micke at all.

"Where's Micke?"

"He's gone over to the other side," said Sausage.

"The other side of the lake?" I asked.

"To Weine's troop," said Lennart, who had overheard us.

"I never thought he'd . . ." I said mainly to myself.

I was surprised that Micke had changed sides. Why did he want to be on the wrong side? He wasn't stupid.

"Maybe they've taken over the castle," said Sausage.

"Then we'll take it back again," I said.

But I didn't think they had. Not yet. Not Weine's troop.

13

s we walked along the path, it struck me that the castle was the only thing I had left that I could still call mine. It seemed that everything had been taken away from me this summer bit by bit. It started with the bag of Twist. It could have all been planned from the start by the grown-ups. They wanted to show us who was in charge. As if we didn't already know.

But they didn't just want to be in charge. They wanted to own us. You can do whatever you want with something you own. You can even smash it to pieces.

That's the way it was. That's why they'd ordered all the children to go searching through the forest for Kerstin, and why they hadn't called the police. The police might ask the children questions. And we might say things the grown-ups didn't want anybody to know.

Would any of us ever get away from here? I could see the back of Kerstin's neck in front of me. It was thin and white. The sun had disappeared and the colors had crept back underneath the moss and into the trees. Everything in the forest was becoming black and white. Then I saw the outline of the castle. We were home.

"It looks deserted," said Janne.

"Good." I went to the moat. There was mud at the bottom but no water. "Maybe they've been here and gone."

"What should we do now?" asked Sausage.

"Let's make a fire," said the boy with the hat. "It'll be hard, but we can do it."

The explorers had brought the perch with them. I lifted one of them. It must have weighed more than half a pound and was nice and solid.

Lennart and Sausage went to gather some twigs and branches. I flattened out the ash in the campfire. Everything inside the ring of stones was cold now. I wondered again who had been there earlier and made a fire. Maybe Micke with Weine's troop. I still couldn't understand how he could change sides. Was it because I hadn't been a good enough leader? Had I left them too much on their own? Been too unyielding with Matron and the grown-ups? Maybe I should have been smarter from the start. Been more laid back. Said nothing about the Twist bag. Eaten everything that crawled around on my plate in the mess hall.

A quarter of an hour later we had a good fire burning. We sat around it in a circle and watched the flames. Kerstin was sitting next to me. I had been waiting for the right moment to ask her what had happened, but that moment hadn't come yet.

"Won't they see the fire?" asked the archer.

"No," said Janne. "We're too far away. And the wind's blowing in the other direction."

The archer looked around.

"This is a nice place you've built."

Nobody answered, but it was nice to hear.

"We've got a reserve castle," said Janne. "We can go there later. They'll never find that place." He looked around. "The walls are higher than they are here."

"Do you have a place of your own?" asked Sausage. "An encampment or something like that?"

"Only the canoe," said the one with the hat. "That's our encampment."

"Explorers are nomads," said the archer. "We move around all the time."

"Samurai are nomads too," said Sausage. "We keep moving like the waves of the sea. That's why we're also called 'wave men.'"

Sausage looked at me. I nodded. Maybe it sounded a bit strange right now, but it was true.

"You build pretty well for being nomads," said the archer with a laugh. "But there's not much in the way of waves in that moat."

"We need some place to keep coming back to," I said. "You have your canoe. We've got our castle."

The one with the hat nodded and started counting heads sitting around the fire.

"There are five of you here from the summer camp," he said when he'd finished counting. "They must have finished eating supper by now. And you're not there."

"That's true," said Sausage cheerfully.

"So what'll they do? Send out a search party? Or phone the cops?" said the one with the hat.

I looked at Kerstin again. As long as she was here, they would wait as long as possible before calling the cops. I think Matron and Christian realized that she was with us. Pretty soon they'd come back here to look for us but not until it had gotten darker.

For now Kerstin was safe, but that wouldn't last forever. We weren't safe ourselves. They were crazy and it wasn't just because they were grown-ups.

"Aren't you missing too?" asked Janne.

"Mom and Dad won't mind as long as I make it back

before school starts," said the archer.

"Wow," said Sausage.

"For me, it's enough if I'm home the day before my confirmation," said the one with the hat.

"You're gonna get confirmed?" asked Sausage.

"No," he replied and burst out laughing.

"Then you'll never get home," said Sausage.

"I've got the canoe. I can paddle wherever I want. Have you seen what the world looks like? There's water everywhere." He looked at me. "I can paddle to Japan. You can come with me if you want."

"But we were going to go to Missouri," said the archer. "Follow the Missouri River all the way."

"That's on the way to Japan."

"No it isn't."

It depends on which way you go," said the one with the hat. "On second thought, no it doesn't. The world is round. You always get to where you're going if you keep at it long enough."

"He's always like this," said the archer looking at me. "Should we grill the fish now?"

I can't say that everybody got full, but we all had some and it was the best thing I'd tasted all summer—along with the hot dogs the lady at the stand had given us. We didn't have any salt but I doubt anyone cared. I asked Kerstin what she thought and she said it tasted great. She didn't say anything apart from that. She started shivering again but only for a few seconds.

Sausage ate some of the skin as well—those pieces that were crisp enough.

"This only made me even more hungry," he complained.

"We've got dessert," I said. "The bag of Twist."

"Do we dare open it?" asked Sausage.

"Why shouldn't we?" I said. "It's mine, isn't it?"

"Twist," said the archer. "I haven't had Twist since we found a bag at the supermarket a few weeks ago."

"Those weren't Twists," said the one with the hat. "They were some other kind of chocolates. And we didn't exactly find them."

"Same difference."

"I'll go get it," I said. I stood up and walked over to the hiding place.

It was empty.

The glow from the embers was like a red eye staring up at the dark blue sky. Everybody sat there thinking about chocolate. You couldn't start talking about chocolate and then expect everybody to stop thinking about it.

I had been robbed of my bag of Twist twice. I don't know which time was worse.

"Weine," said Sausage. "Or Micke."

"Probably both of them," said Janne. "I'll have their heads for this."

"No," I said, "they're mine."

"Did you know that it was the white man who started taking scalps?" said the one with the hat. "At least in the American Northeast. The state of Minnesota. Cheyenne country."

"Swedes," I said.

"Huh?"

"I'm talking about the whites. It was mainly Swedes who emigrated to America, wasn't it? To Minnesota."

"You may be right."

"So it was Swedes who taught the Indians to take scalps."

"I don't know if they *taught* them exactly," said the one with the hat. "It must have been a pretty painful thing to learn!"

Somebody burst out laughing.

Kerstin started crying.

"He . . . chased me in there."

She had started talking at last. I knew she would. At first her teeth were chattering like castanets.

"He told me to go in . . . in . . . to . . . the room."

"What for?" asked Sausage.

"Shut up, Sausage," I said.

"Which room?" asked Janne.

"That . . . office. The one that Matron has."

"Were you alone?" I asked.

"Yes . . . by then. Ann was outside but he said he wanted to talk to me about something."

"Was he alone?"

"Uh . . . yes."

"Where was Matron?"

"She was in the hall."

"So she knew that Christian wanted to talk to you in the office?"

"Yes, she saw us."

"She saw Christian and you going into her office?"

Kerstin nodded.

"What did she say?"

"She didn't say anything. She . . . started walking away. I just caught sight of her turning her back on me . . . on us . . . and heading outside."

"Then what happened?"

Kerstin's teeth started chattering again.

"I jump . . . jumped out of the window," she said.

She didn't want to say what had happened in the office, but she had told us the important part—that she'd escaped. That was starting to look like the only way out of this place.

"I think we'd better get out of here now," said Janne.

We went deeper into the woods. It had grown darker, and it felt like we were walking deeper into the night. There were no rules that applied any more. There were less than two weeks to go before the summer camp closed down for the season. But not even that applied now.

The wall looked like a dinosaur's spine in the dim light. The reserve castle was not much more than the wall and a lean-to where you could shelter from the wind. I could see the field and the edge of the trees on the other side. The field was like a lake. I thought of the explorers' canoe. The grown-ups might have found it by now, but the explorers didn't seem worried. They had become a part of our troop. Maybe they were tired of being on their own. There's strength in numbers.

"How many of them are there?" asked the archer out of

the blue. He seemed to be reading my thoughts. "Grown-ups at the camp?"

I thought for a moment. Matron and the counselors. And Christian. And the cook.

"Seven altogether."

"And we are . . ."

"Nine," I said, "with you two and Kerstin."

"Good. What weapons have you got?"

"Only the ones we took with us from the castle."

"No hidden supplies here?"

"Not yet. We've thought about it."

"There's one other thing," said Lennart, who was standing beside me. "Weine's troop. And Micke."

"What about them?" asked the one with the hat.

"They're our enemies too," said Lennart.

"Do you think they'd fight on the same side as the grown-ups?" asked the archer.

"Are we really going to fight?" wondered Sausage.

"Haven't you understood anything?" said Janne.

"We can't trust anybody apart from ourselves," I said. "Everyone standing here."

Although not everybody was standing. Kerstin had sat down inside the lean-to and was gazing out over the field, as if she thought somebody might approach from that direction. But if they did come, it would be from inside the woods behind us.

I was sure of one thing. This wasn't a game—if it ever had been. They wouldn't call the police. They would try to catch Kerstin first. And us. I felt my sword. It was just as heavy and sharp as before. The sword was ready. But was I ready? Was the troop ready? If we really were samurai, we were ready for anything. I heard a sound. It could have been a twig snapping. Sound travels a long way in a silent forest. Then I heard another noise.

"There's somebody out there," whispered Janne, nodding toward the trees.

We couldn't see anything moving. We waited, but there were no more sounds.

"What is it?" whispered Sausage.

"We don't need to whisper," I said. "They know we're here."

"It could be a deer," said the archer.

He had his bow ready with an arrow in place. He was prepared to shoot at anything that emerged from the trees. The point of the arrow was as sharp as a needle. Anybody hit by that would be in trouble.

There was another crack that was louder this time. Whoever was moving around out there wasn't trying to creep up on us. It must be an animal that, maybe, was heading away from us.

"Kenny!"

I gave a start. We all did. If it was an animal, it could talk.

I could see something moving over by a tree twenty yards away. It was a white hand waving at us.

"Don't shoot. It's Micke!"

He must have seen the archer. The arrow was aimed straight at the tree. The archer didn't lower his bow.

I recognized Micke's voice, but that didn't mean I trusted him.

"Are you on your own?" I shouted.

"I'm here with Weine. And his troop."

"What do you want?"

"We want peace." I thought I caught a glimpse of his face. "We've come in peace."

"You've betrayed us, Micke."

"Can I come and explain?"

"Where are the others?"

"They're waiting a little farther back in the trees. Kenny! You've got to let me come up and talk to you. It's important. Life and death, Kenny!"

I listened for Weine and his gang but couldn't hear anything. No disturbed birds or other forest animals. If Weine's soldiers were there, they were very skilled at moving through trees.

"Lower your bow a little," I said to the archer, "but keep the arrow in."

"I'm coming out now," said Micke. "Don't shoot."

"Hold your sword over your head," I said.

It was strange, but I was pleased to see him. But we were still keeping a close eye on him. Nobody cheered when he made it to the wall. Micke kept an eye on the archer who was standing at the ready, but he didn't ask who he was, nor who the one with the hat was either. He asked about somebody else.

"Is Kerstin here?"

"Why do you ask?"

"You should see what it's like at the camp, Kenny!"

"What's that got to do with her?" I asked.

"What do you want?" It was Kerstin's voice.

I turned around. She was standing next to the lean-to with the blanket wrapped around her.

"Kerstin!" He took a step forward, still with his sword above his head. "You're here!" He looked at me. "Thank God."

"What's going on at the camp?"

"Can I lower the sword?" he asked.

"Put it on the ground."

The archer was aiming at Micke as he put the sword down at my feet. I didn't want to look at it. I didn't like it when somebody was forced to lay down their sword.

"The other one too," I said.

He took out his *wakizashi* without saying a word and put it down beside the *katana*. He was almost naked now, but it didn't seem to bother him—at least not yet.

"What's going on?" I asked again.

"They seem to be out of their minds," he said. "Matron and Christian. Especially Matron."

"What are they doing?"

"All the children have been forbidden to leave their dormitories. Nobody's allowed out."

"What's so strange about that?" asked Janne, who was standing next to Micke. "It's always like that."

"But now they've put out guards. Matron and Christian are patrolling outside. And the cook, too, I think. They're going in and out of the main building. If you get in their way, you won't make it out alive."

"But you made it out. And Weine and his gang," I said.

"Exactly," said the archer.

"We never went in," said Micke. "We slipped away after the search party got back."

"How do you know they put up guards then?"

"Ann," he said. "She hid under the steps when they ordered everybody to go upstairs. I don't know how she did it. You'll have to ask her."

"Is Ann here?" I heard Kerstin ask. She'd been standing behind me the whole time. "Where's Ann?"

"She's waiting with the others," said Micke.

"What do you want us to do?" I asked. "You and Weine."

"We have to join forces and fight them," said Micke. "We won't be able to do it if we don't." He looked at Kerstin. "There's something damn—very strange about Matron. More than usual. And Christian too."

"Have they called the police?" asked Janne. "Do you know? Reported her missing?"

"Not as far as I know," said Micke. "But we can ask Ann."

14

They came out of the trees one by one with Weine leading the way. This time he didn't look like he wanted to trip anybody up. He was looking around all the time as if expecting to be attacked at any moment.

"Who are they?" asked the one with the hat. "Are they samurai too?"

"No," I said. "They're just bandits."

"Do you trust them?"

"About as far as I trust the grown-ups."

"Then maybe we should start disarming them?"

"We can't keep them as prisoners," I said. "If we did, we wouldn't be able to do anything else apart from guarding them."

Weine had reached the wall. He looked at me but wasn't smiling. He looked scared. But it wasn't me or us he was afraid of. He looked around again to see if whoever he was scared of had been following him and was lurking in the shadows.

"So you found your way here," I said.

Weine gestured toward Micke.

"It was necessary," said Micke.

"What's so necessary?" I asked.

"That we join forces," said Weine.

"How are the other kids, the little ones?" I asked.

"Locked inside."

"What are they doing to them?"

Weine shrugged. "They're scared."

I saw Ann cross the path and run up to Kerstin.

"I've been so worried," said Ann.

Kerstin hugged her without speaking.

I went over to them.

"Ann?" I said.

She looked up. I hardly recognized her close-up. Her face looked older. It seemed like she'd aged ten years over the last few hours. Her brown hair was glued to her forehead as though she'd swum here. She wasn't cocky anymore, that was for sure.

"I heard you went and hid," I said.

"Yes . . . under the steps."

"Didn't anybody look there?"

"No. They were in such a hurry."

"To do what?"

"To lock everybody inside."

"Why did they want to do that?"

"To stop any more of them running away, I think."

"Why would anybody else want to run away?"

I felt like a detective interrogating her.

"They were . . . trying to hit us," said Ann. "Chr-Christian and Matron. They were going crazy."

She looked at Kerstin when she mentioned Christian's name. Kerstin looked away.

"What about the counselors?"

"They were gone by then," she replied. "They drove off in a car."

"A car? Is there a dance tonight?"

"I don't know."

"But Matron and Christian are still there?"

"Yes. And the cook."

"They're really crazy," said Weine. "Worse than before. Out of their minds."

"Well, you should know," said Janne. "They're buddies of yours."

"They are not!"

"Why aren't they out in the woods?" I asked. "Why didn't they follow you?"

"They're making plans right now," said Micke.

"What are they thinking of doing?" wondered Janne.

"Maybe they're going to call in some more grown-ups," said Micke.

"Holy crap," said Weine.

"I thought you liked grown-ups, Weine," said Janne.

Weine reached for the sword he had in his belt. It was a clumsy sword—like a little kid's.

"Cut it out!" I shouted.

Weine let go of the handle.

"I don't want him to say things like that," he said.

"Why should they want to call in more grown-ups when they've let the counselors leave?" I asked.

"Maybe the counselors are too nice for them," Micke looked at me. "Maybe they want some other ones."

"No," I said, "they don't want any more. They don't want any more witnesses."

"Witnesses to what?" Sausage asked.

I didn't answer.

Nobody spoke for a few seconds. I could hear the wind in the treetops. It had picked up even more over the last half-hour. The sky was darker. It felt almost like an autumn night. All the faces had turned into white patches.

"So what do we do now?" asked Sausage finally.

I looked at Janne and then at Lennart. Sausage looked

at me. Were we all thinking the same thing? That Weine had been sent out by the grown-ups as a spy? I eyed Micke up and down. Could he be a part of it too? In that case, he'd become a grown-up as well in just a few days.

But I noticed how he kept glancing back into the trees with a worried look in his eyes. He didn't look like a deserter. Deserters' eyes aren't like that.

"Guess we'd better rescue them," said the archer from the other side of the wall. He raised his bow. "This'll take me pretty far." He pointed at my *katana*. "And you have your swords."

"We ought to be able to take them by surprise," said Micke. "They're not expecting us to come back."

It felt like everybody was looking at me. I could see the white patches glowing like dim lights in the darkening evening. Soon it would be night. Then what would happen? We had to do something. I tried to think—think really hard about what we should do. And why we should do it.

I understood that we were in danger. We all did. The kids at the camp were in danger. But I wasn't quite sure how.

"We have to do something, Kenny." It was Kerstin's voice. "We can't just hang around here."

She had let go of Ann and had come toward me. She looked like a ghost that had transformed into a human being. Her face was no longer a white patch.

"I feel better now," she said.

I think she even gave a little smile.

Maybe it was just something she said. When we were sitting in the lean-to, she didn't look like she was feeling all that great. But she wasn't silent any more. And it wasn't silent outside either. I could hear sword striking against sword. Micke and Janne were practicing. *Kendo.* The way of the sword.

At one time, there were hundreds of sword-fighting schools all over Japan. It was always taken seriously. Nobody treated it like a sport.

The explorers had each been given a sword, too, but I knew the archer wouldn't use his if fighting started.

"How are you feeling?" I asked Kerstin.

"I told you, I'm all right."

"Have you got . . . any pain?"

"No. Not physical," she said looking me in the eye. "He, Christian . . . tried to . . . but I got away."

I didn't know what to say.

"Have you got any more swords?" she asked after a pause.

We could hear the sword practice continuing behind the lean-to. She stood up and so did I. We could see the outline of the swordsmen against the sky and the forest. It was like a theater stage with cardboard cutouts. Shadow theater.

"I want a sword."

"Then you'll have to practice," I said.

"Give me one, then."

We practiced in the clearing. She was fast. Sausage and I had made the *bokken* she was using at the same time we'd made his. It was a twin.

"This is *kenjutsu*," I said as I slashed through the air alongside Kerstin. "It means 'the art of the sword.'"

I showed her a few of the sixteen different sword moves that the samurai used. They each had their own name: "Thunder," "Wheel Attack," "Pea-Slicer." The Chinese had even more names for how you could strike with your sword—names that sounded like poems: "Tigers lurking at the front door;" "The black dragon strikes with its tail;" "The white snake stings with its tongue;" "Hold the moon in your hands;" "Stir up dust in the wind;" "Paint a red stain between the eyebrows;" "Turn around and hang up the golden bell;" "Pick stars with a hovering hand."

We took a break. I had started sweating. I could see that Kerstin was sweating too. Her hair had gotten darker from the sweat, and some strands were stuck to her ears. She was starting to look like a warrior.

"Do we really stand a chance?" she asked all of a sudden.

"Of defending ourselves? Yes."

"But if we attack? We're going to have to attack, aren't we?"

"Yes. We have to find out what's going on over there, anyway."

"Can we do that without attacking?"

"We won't know until we've checked it out," I said.

"Isn't it time we did, then?"

Kerstin, Janne, Micke, and I went. We didn't want to leave both Micke and Weine with the others after what had happened before. Plus, Micke was one of the last ones to leave the camp. And Kerstin the first. We needed both of them in the advance guard. Lennart was left in command of the rest of the troop including the explorers. He didn't object when I said that he was in charge. He was calm, and calmness was what we needed.

When we reached the castle, it looked like war had already broken out. The wall was destroyed in the middle, and two of the towers had been pulled down.

"Somebody's been walking in the moat," said Janne.

It could have been one or several people. All the footprints were from grown-up feet.

"What's the point of trying to destroy the castle?" Kerstin wondered.

"No point at all," said Janne.

"They don't want us to have anything to come back to,"
I said.

"Do they know that we're going to attack?" asked Kerstin.

I tried to picture their faces in my mind's eye: Matron,
Christian. What did they look like right now? Were they
waiting for the enemy?

We continued slowly on toward the camp. The forest was
the darkest place on earth at this moment, but even so, it
wasn't difficult to find our way. We knew these woods inside
out. We'd made most of the paths ourselves.

After a quarter of an hour, I could see a glimmer through
the trees and then another. It was the moon glinting on the
lake.

Soon we would be able to see the mess hall windows.

We stopped. A bird cried out over the water. It sounded
like a warning, but I didn't know for whom or for what. I
hoped the bird was on our side.

"Wait here," I said, and I set off toward the camp.

The moon was lighting up the buildings. I could see one
of the walls a hundred yards away. There was light coming
from two of the windows. It must be Matron's office. I paused,
but I couldn't hear any voices. I was still too far away. The
bird cried out again. It was closer now.

I crawled through the grass to the main gates and snuck

behind the big stone. There was a light shining beneath the door of the barracks where the counselors slept. I saw somebody come out, walk across the grounds, and vanish behind the other side of the main building. I couldn't see who it was.

There were no lights on in the dormitories facing this way. It was nighttime, but I don't think the kids were asleep. Maybe some of them were looking out the windows right now. I didn't want them to see me. Not yet.

Suddenly I heard a cry. It wasn't the bird this time.

15

I heard a loud *thwack*. Something hard hitting something soft. I heard a voice cry out again followed by a shout that wasn't quite a cry. Then I heard two voices coming from inside the building. It sounded like they came from a grown-up and a kid. Then it went so quiet that I could hear the sound of birds' wings through the night wind. The birds flew without screeching. They were waiting. The fog floated back and forth out on the lake as if it, too, was waiting. Maybe to envelop us when all of this was over. After the battle.

I looked behind me, but I couldn't see anyone from the advance guard. That was good. It meant no one in the building could see them either. I turned back toward the main building and the barracks, the sheds, the playing field, and the dock by the wash area. I saw all those places and thought about how they'd soon be gone. I was the last one to see it all. I could see a couple of the swings in the moonlight. The moon had come out from behind a cloud that was floating across the sky. It was white everywhere as if it had silently started to snow. I thought the sky was shutting its eyes right now. The swings swayed slowly in the wind as if invisible children were having a final swing.

Something moved in one of the dark windows on the third floor. Maybe it was a kid who'd gathered the courage to peek outside. I didn't know, but I did know that I couldn't stay here any longer. I had to find out more about what was happening in there and what had happened already. Everything was waiting for me to make up my mind.

I felt the right side of my face starting to ache. I lifted my head away from the stone gatepost and moved it back and forth a little until it didn't hurt so much anymore. I shut my eyes, and when I opened them again, the light had been switched out in the barracks. Had the counselors come back, or was there someone else in the barracks? Maybe they had seen me after all. It was time to get moving.

I started crawling through the grass. My face got wet, maybe from the fog sweeping in from the lake and filling the air with water.

Once I'd reached the corner of the building, I stood up cautiously and snuck slowly along the wall facing the lake. No

one in the barracks could see me from here. The advance guard
out in the forest could see me, only now it was a rearguard,
of course. Janne, Micke, and Kerstin were still waiting for a
signal from me. They probably wondered what I was doing.
This may have been the craziest thing I'd ever done. And I'd
done a lot of crazy things.

I saw a light coming from one of the windows. It was
like a flashlight shining toward the lake. The beam seemed to
reach halfway across to the other side. Then it disappeared
into the blackness. For a second I thought I didn't want to
know what had happened here—or what was in the process
of happening. But seconds later I realized that I didn't have
a choice.

I moved slowly toward the light, still hugging the wall. It
smelled of paint even though no one had painted it during
any of the summers I'd been there. Maybe it was because the
paint had started to peel and flake off that I could smell it. A
few flakes got caught in my hair like little feathers. I looked
out at the lake again. I half expected the explorers' canoe to
come gliding into the beam of light from the window.

Maybe it was a mistake that they weren't out on the lake
instead. It made a good observation point from out there,
and mine wasn't quite as good. I had to move closer to the
window. The moonlight was reflected in the glass pane, and
I could see that the window was open. As I got closer, I

started hearing voices—first a mumbling and then words or parts of words.

I was almost right below the window now. I looked up but nobody looked out. It sounded like the people who were talking were standing well inside the room.

"They're not far away. You do realize that, don't you?"

It was Matron's voice, but I almost didn't recognize it because it sounded like it had been squeezed and become thinner.

"How do you know?"

Christian's voice was also hard to recognize. It sounded coarser than usual, thicker, as if he had something in his throat.

"You don't know ANYTHING," he shouted after clearing his throat. "What do YOU know?"

"I kno—" said Matron but broke off in mid-sentence. "What was that?"

"What?"

"I heard something. From outside."

I curled up beneath the window. The only thing I had heard myself was a rumbling far away in the sky. It seemed like the thunder wanted to let us all know that it was there and that it could come back at any moment.

I squeezed myself farther into the shadows.

I heard footsteps in the room and soon a head stuck out

the window. It was like a black cardboard cutout.

I could see the head move.

"There's nothing out here," said Christian.

"I heard something," said Matron's voice.

The thunder rumbled again just as far away as before.

"It's just the thunder," said Christian, and the head disappeared back inside.

I crawled in a little closer. The thunder rumbled yet again. It sounded closer this time.

Matron said something that I didn't hear. It sounded like she had moved farther inside the room, off toward the door.

"It's too late now," said Christian.

Mumble.

"It's TOO LATE, I said."

"If only you had thought about that before." Matron's voice. It sounded thicker now.

This time it was Christian who mumbled. They seemed to be walking around in the room. I thought of how Christian had sat on the merry-go-round and gazed up at the girls' dorm.

"I can only do what I'm already doing," said Matron.

"So I've noticed," said Christian.

"I'm not the one who did it," said Matron.

"You've done enough," answered Christian.

Another mumble. It sounded like Matron.

"Did you hear what I said? Huh? HUH?"

That was Matron.

I heard a smack. A cry.

It was the same smack I had heard over by the gate. The same cry. The same voices.

Then everything suddenly went quiet.

"It's too late," Christian's voice said again.

I waited. I tried to understand what they had been talking about, but no more words came. I did understand that the kids were in danger—that we were all in danger. The door opened at the far end of the room. Christian and Matron were heading outside. What if they were going to check the lake and make sure that there was no one around the building?

I heard heavy footsteps. They were on their way over here! It was fifteen yards down to the lake. There were birch trees that could offer protection by the edge of the water, but I wouldn't have time to make it down there or around the corner; and anyway, I couldn't tell which direction the footsteps were coming from.

There was a fire ladder to the left of the window a few feet from where I was crouching.

I jumped up, grabbed hold of the lowest rung, and was able to pull myself up until I could get my knee around it. It felt like my tendons were being cut off.

I rocked back and forth and managed to grab hold of a rung farther up and then to get my feet up onto the lowest rung. I climbed up the ladder in a flash. It continued all the way up to the roof and ended at the chimney. I leaned in toward the brickwork. It felt rough against my cheek.

I could see in all directions from up here.

I saw the whole lake. It looked like a silver tray in the moonlight. I could see all the way to the opposite shore even though it was dark.

I saw the wash area, the courtyard, the playground, the merry-go-round, the sheds, the barracks—everything.

I saw the gate, and just then a figure came rushing through it. The stubby legs were clearly visible, and the entire suit of armor was gleaming in the moonlight.

It was Sausage.

Sausage had wanted to come along when the advance guard set off. He had wanted to be at the very front at least once. He wanted to prove something—that he was just as tough as anyone else. I told him that he had already done that the night we snuck out from the camp and went to the castle. That had been brave of Sausage and he knew it.

Now he wanted to be brave again.

He was dressed for battle. He held his sword at the ready as he ran. He shouted something—a battle cry that echoed across the lake behind me. I didn't know Sausage could yell that loud. He yelled again. Birds flew from their nests. I heard the sound of their wings around me.

Sausage ran toward the building I was hiding on. He couldn't see me. I tried to call out, but he couldn't hear me through his own yelling. There was no one running next to him or behind him. No one in the troop had stopped him. He must have come through the forest from another direction.

I heard a door fly open down below and then footsteps on the stairs. I leaned forward for support against the chimney, but I couldn't see anything. Sausage had almost reached the building. Then he disappeared from view. I heard him shouting, but that was suddenly cut short. Then I heard a sigh—or a whispering—as though the sound was making its way up to the roof. There it was again creeping along the roof tiles. It was a scary sound. And then it, too, disappeared.

Then I heard voices from the other side of the building. I slid slowly down the roof toward the rain gutter. I looked over the edge and saw the beam of light from the open window. Shadows moved around for a while and then disappeared. I started to climb down. I thought of Sausage and the silence after his shouts. It was a terrible silence. It was worse than his yelling.

Halfway down the ladder that was fixed to the wall, I heard the voices more clearly. I recognized them.

"What have you DONE?" That was Christian.

"He just came rushing at me. You saw that."

"Is that . . . is that his sword?"

"Who else's would it be? It's not mine anyway."

"Is he . . . is he . . ."

It was Christian who was asking. I felt the terror surging up inside me just as palpably as if it had hit me while flapping by in the night.

I jumped the final feet down to the ground and landed softly. I didn't hear what Matron said in answer to Christian's question, but I understood that they had captured Sausage.

Out of nowhere, a bolt of lightning lit up the entire sky.

16

A split second after the flash of lightning there was a deafening crash, and in the next second another bolt of lightning struck. It was like standing in the middle of an explosion. Everything was lit up brighter and sharper than in the middle of the day.

I waited for a third flash of lightning but I didn't see one, and there were no more thunderclaps.

I rushed back to the gate. There was no time now to creep and crawl through the grass.

There was no one at the edge of the forest. Had everyone disappeared? A hand was waving, making a white circle in the darkness by a tree fifteen feet away. I ran over and Kerstin stepped out from behind it.

"We were so worried!"

"Where are the others?"

"Janne's run back to the rest of the troop. Micke is down by the lake, I think."

"What's he doing there?"

"I don't know. Maybe he's scouting around."

Scouting, I thought. *Was he trying to find a position of attack? Or was he planning to ambush us? Could we trust him or not?*

"Did you see Sausage?" I asked.

"Yeah, my god, he just rushed right past us before we could stop him."

"Did you try?"

"We didn't get a chance. He just rushed right past us, and then he was inside the grounds and we couldn't run after him. There weren't enough of us. That's why Janne is getting the others."

"Didn't you call out to Sausage?"

"We tried but he didn't hear us. He didn't seem to hear anything."

"Did you see what happened to him after that?

"No. He disappeared behind the building." She pointed at the building and then looked at me. "Why did he do that? It was completely idiotic. Pure suicide."

Suicide, I thought. A samurai always has to be ready to commit suicide. But not just whenever and by whatever means. If it's going to happen, it has to be a *seppuku* or *harakiri* as it's also called. That means "belly cut." You slice open your belly with the little knife. *Hara* is Japanese for belly. *Kiri* means cut.

There's a reason why samurai do it that way. The stomach is the center of the body and the soul. When the stomach doesn't work, neither does anything else. All samurai know that. But to rush straight into the arms of Matron wasn't *harakiri*. It was just stupid.

"What do we do now?" asked Kerstin.

I didn't answer. I was still thinking about Sausage.

"We have to do something!" she continued. "We can't just stand around here anymore. I can't stand around here anymore. We have to save Sausage. And the others."

"Have you seen any of them?" I asked.

"They've looked out the window a few times, but it's dark."

We heard a noise behind us and turned around. It was Micke.

"They dragged Sausage in through the main door," he said.

"You saw that?"

"I was standing down at the tree by the water."

"Did you see who it was?"

"Matron. I saw Christian too."

"What did they do with him?"

"Hit him with a stick," said Micke. "Matron just whacked him. He fell like a rock."

"My god," said Kerstin.

"Isn't Janne back?" Micke asked.

Just then we heard a branch crack in the forest. Micke grabbed his sword. We heard more cracking sounds, and then saw a figure emerge from the forest, and then another. The troop was assembled.

We snuck forward in a long line with fifteen feet between us. We covered the whole distance from the edge of the forest to the edge of the lake.

Weine was at the far end of the right flank and Micke was farthest to the left, closest to the forest. I was in the middle with Kerstin next to me. We all had our swords ready. Kerstin was breathing so loudly that anyone nearby could hear her.

I had just seen a light flare up and disappear again in a window on the first floor. I looked up at the sky, but there was no more lightning. The sky was completely black. There was no light left. The moon had disappeared behind the blackness too. We could hardly see each other anymore.

Then there was another short flicker of light.

"It's on fire!"

I recognized Janne's voice in the darkness. He was walking on my right.

"A fire's broken out below the dormitory!"

"That's the kitchen!" shouted Micke.

I saw a glimmer of light again, but this time it didn't disappear. It grew. First the light flickered in the window farthest to the left, then in the window next to it, and then in a third. We weren't sneaking forward anymore. We ran up to the building as fast as we could. One of the trees outside the kitchen had caught fire. The trunk grew at an angle toward the building, and the flames were licking their way down the trunk and in through the open kitchen window.

Kerstin ran past me. She was faster than I was. Someone wrenched open a window upstairs.

"Help! Help!"

A face appeared. It was speckled from the fire. I recognized one of the little boys but couldn't remember his name.

"Help! We can't get out!"

I tried to judge the distance from the window down to the ground.

"They've locked us inside!"

It was at least twenty feet to the ground—maybe twenty-five. Those who tried to jump would break every bone in their body including their neck. There was no soft grass underneath the windows, just a few benches that we wouldn't have time to pull out of the way.

"Is it burning inside the room?" I shouted.

"No," someone answered up there.

"It was struck by lightning!" I shouted.

I could see flames in the windows in front of me and there was a strong smell of smoke. Kerstin was headed toward the mess hall.

"Kerstin!"

She didn't turn around when I shouted so I started running after her. At the same time, I saw the explorers come running across the grounds.

"It's on fire!" shouted the archer.

"I know! We have to get everyone out!"

"Where are they?"

"Up there," I shouted and pointed as I ran.

I had almost reached the steps to the mess hall. "Try to put out the fire!"

In the next second, I was up the steps and I threw myself inside. The explorers came in right behind me. I saw Kerstin rush up the stairs to the dormitory and disappear around the corner.

"In there!" I shouted and pointed at the kitchen. Smoke was coming through the doorway, but there wasn't a lot. "Maybe it hasn't really caught yet."

"Maybe we can put it out," said the one with the hat. "There's water in there."

I heard Kerstin yell something from upstairs.

The explorers ran toward the kitchen. Kerstin's face appeared from around the corner.

"They're all locked inside the same room!"

"We're trying to put out the fire down here!"

"Where's the key?" she shouted.

Yeah, where? *Wherever Matron is,* I thought.

I heard voices behind me. The rest of the troop stormed in.

"We have to put out the fire!" shouted Lennart, who stopped next to me. "We have to get everyone out of here!"

"Help the explorers in the kitchen," I shouted. "Ann, Weine, and Mats, help Kerstin upstairs."

The three of them rushed up the steps. The others ran off toward the kitchen.

I thought of Matron's office. That's where the keys would be. That must be where they took Sausage. I ran down the hallway. The door to the office was shut. I stopped outside and tried to slow my breathing. It was quiet inside. I didn't smell any fire here and I couldn't hear anything from upstairs anymore.

I grasped the handle and pressed down. The door was unlocked and I pushed it open.

Nothing moved inside. All the lamps seemed to be on and there was light everywhere. The window was open. Outside, the lake was glittering and twinkling. I could see Matron's desk. There was only one thing on the desk: my bag of Twist.

"I knew you'd come."

Matron's voice startled me.

When I turned around, she was standing in the middle of the room. She must have been waiting behind the door when I opened it. Now she blocked the exit. She was holding out her arms like swords. But the only sword in here was the one I had in my belt. I touched the hilt. It was cold. The cold made me calmer.

"The kitchen's on fire," I said.

"I haven't noticed anything," said Matron without moving. She looked straight at me, but it seemed like her eyes couldn't see. It looked like she was sleepwalking. Her voice sounded like it came from a dream.

"The kids are locked upstairs," I continued. "We've got to get them out quickly."

She didn't respond.

"Where are the keys?"

She didn't respond to that either.

"WHERE ARE THE KEYS?"

When I raised my voice, something happened to her. Her eyes seemed to see again. She shuddered as if she suddenly felt cold.

"It wasn't me," she said.

"What?"

"I wasn't me," she repeated. "I've never done anyone any harm, have I?"

She took a step forward.

"Right, Tommy? Kenny? You've always had it good here with me, haven't you? You've been here a few summers. You know, Kenny!"

I heard shouting from the kitchen. Maybe the fire was spreading. Maybe they couldn't make it down the stairs anymore.

"Just give me the keys," I said.

I still felt calm, but at the same time I was very worried. Now I was being tested as a samurai.

"You can have the keys. If you don't say anything."

She took another step.

"About what happened. About that girl."

"What happened?" I asked.

"It was nothing," she said. "Nothing happened."

Just like always around here, I thought. Nothing that happened ever actually happened. Not even when the worst happened did they ever say that anything had happened.

"Then there's nothing I have to say anything about," I said, "if nothing happened."

"Nobody's going to believe you anyway, Kenny."

She was holding her bunch of keys in her hand. There were four or five of them attached to a little chain. It looked thin. She dangled them from her forefinger.

"Then it doesn't make any difference whether I say anything or not," I said.

"But it's so unnecessary to say a bunch of lies about someone who hasn't done anything," she said.

I could smell the smoke. She must have smelled it too. But it was more important for her to buy my silence with those keys than it was to get everyone to safety and to keep the camp from burning down.

In that moment, it struck me that she was never going to give me those keys. Then I heard a heavy pounding upstairs. It was resonating through the ceiling. I guessed that Kerstin and the others were trying to break down the door to the dormitory, but it would be difficult. The doors here were made of solid wood—just like in a prison.

The pounding stopped. The smell of smoke was still in the air but all was quiet again as though Matron and I were the only ones here. Somehow it had always felt that way. It was Kenny against Matron. There was no Christian here. I hadn't even had time to think about where he had gone. I hadn't had time to think about where Sausage was.

The keys rattled. Matron was still dangling them from her finger. I heard the pounding from upstairs again, and it sounded like someone was screaming for help. Matron stood just a few steps away from me. There were maybe ten feet between us.

I drew my sword. She took a long step toward me, like a lunge, and in that exact split second, I threw myself forward and chopped the key chain off half an inch below Matron's finger. The keys fell to the ground as if in slow motion. I saw Matron slowly raise her finger and look at it.

There wasn't so much as a drop of blood on her finger. The chain still hung there like a thin worm. It would fall off in a few seconds, but first, the keys hit the floor. I put my sword back, bent down, and gathered up all the keys. Then I ran for the door, past Matron who was still standing there staring at her finger.

The mess hall was full of smoke. I heard someone coughing. When I turned around, I saw the cook sitting at one of the long mess hall tables. It must have been the first time she'd ever sat there. She coughed again and looked up, but she didn't appear to see me. Maybe it was the smoke, maybe something else. She looked down at the table again and shook her head.

I ran up the stairs. The troop had managed to smash a hole in the door, but it was too little. They had used a small table as a battering ram.

"I've got the keys," I said. "Get out of the way!"

After two failed attempts, the third key fit. We got the door open and the kids inside tried to rush out all at the same time.

"Take it easy!" shouted Lennart. "Is everyone okay?"

It smelled of smoke in the room but not too much.

Weine, Janne, and I quickly checked to make sure that no one had passed out inside.

"Go down the stairs," said Lennart.

He was my deputy now. He was doing a good job.

"How's it going with the fire in the kitchen?" I asked.

"It's under control," he answered.

"How about Sausage?"

"I don't know," he said. "That's what I'm going to find out now."

Matron was gone when I got back to the office. It was still just as light in there. I walked around to the other side of the desk. Sausage was lying on the floor with his back to me. I bent over and gently grasped his shoulder, but he seemed lifeless. I didn't see any blood.

"Sausage?" I said but got no answer. He didn't open his eyes.

They didn't seem completely closed when I looked more

closely. I tried to hear if he was breathing. As I leaned in, he opened his eyes.

"Kenny!"

"Sausage!"

"I saw the bag of Twist, Kenny!"

The archer came toward us in the mess hall. Sausage had difficulty walking. He had been hit in the head and was pretty dizzy.

"Matron whacked me," he said.

"You're alive, anyway," said the archer, patting him on the shoulder.

The smoke had thinned a little. I couldn't see the cook.

"Where is she?" I asked as I pointed at the mess hall table. The archer understood.

"Outside somewhere," he answered. "I saw that old Matron woman rush outside, too, a moment ago."

"What are they doing?"

"No idea."

"How's it going with the fire?"

"Under control."

"Let me see."

We stood in the kitchen. Here, too, the smoke was clearing and becoming regular air. I could see out the window. The fog was floating across the lake as though the smoke had moved out there.

"The lightning really hit hard," said the archer, and he pointed at the wall beyond the stove.

I could see a black hole next to the window where the fire had made its way inside from the tree. There was still a bit of fire left—like little tongues. If we left the kitchen without putting it out completely, the place would be engulfed in flames within an hour. The entire building was made of wood, and the fire would spread from the kitchen in a few minutes.

All of a sudden a larger tongue of flame shot out from the wall.

The archer bent down over the water bucket.

Janne came into the kitchen. He was holding the banner with our coat of arms: the circle with the two lines that were as black as the soot on the walls.

I thought about what Janne had said once when we were sitting in the castle. If the camp didn't exist, he had said, then we could stay here as long as we wanted. But it does exist, I had said. It's over there behind the trees. If there were no camp. If it didn't exist at all. The camp doesn't exist. The camp is no more.

The archer raised the bucket of water.

"Put it down," I said.

In the shadows from the fire, everyone looked like warriors. We moved around the bonfire in a wide circle. Everything became ten times bigger in the shadows against the sky, the forest, and the lake. It was like a theater show of cardboard cutouts—shadow figures—just like when we trained for battle. Our long and narrow banners were sharp silhouettes against the sky that had almost turned white from the fire.

Kerstin, Sausage, Ann, Lennart, Micke, Janne, and I stood silently watching the fire swallow up the camp. Nobody said anything. The explorers had gone to check on their canoe. Weine and his troop guarded Matron and the cook, who were sitting petrified in the grass behind the counselors' barracks. What was it that I had heard Christian say? *It's all too late.* Christian himself had disappeared.

Matron had gone mute and so had the cook. I had asked Matron about Christian but had got no answer.

I looked at her. She looked at the fire with the same vacant stare she had had in her office.

I could hear the sirens through the forest and across the lake.

"Here they come," said Janne.

I began to make out headlights among the trees.

"A bit late now," said Micke and smiled.

But it wasn't just the fire department I had called from Matron's office. When the police car turned in through the front gate as the first car in a long line of vehicles, I walked out and waved to it.

17

It's long past midnight now. Morning, you could say. There's not much more to tell. The explorers found Christian as he was swimming out toward the middle of the lake. It was when they went to get their canoe to paddle a few of the younger kids over to the other beach. Christian had swum out there in the moonlight and then started to sink like a stone. The explorers put a rope around his chest and dragged him back. They saved his life, of course, and I guess every life is worth saving, both the good ones and the bad. If you save the bad, they have to think about what they've done. They're not saved by death. That's what I think. And maybe they can change. I believe most people can change. I know I did.

Christian didn't say anything while he was lying on the beach. There was no room for any words amidst all the spitting and coughing from the water in his lungs. He looked scared when he finally raised his head and looked at the kids standing around. He seemed small. Like the smallest person there. The smallest person in the world.

No one else said anything either. There was nothing more to say.

I looked at Kerstin. She seemed calm. She was going to be okay. She had already had a long talk with a woman police officer, or at least it seemed like a long talk. They'd been sitting in a police car, and the police officer gave her a hug when they stepped out of the car. I knew there were going to be more talks for Kerstin in the coming days—maybe a lot. They were going to take care of her. The police officer looked nice—old but nice. Maybe she was even over thirty.

Kerstin's mom was coming in the morning, and Kerstin would be going home in a couple of days. Christian would be going to jail, or the nut house, or both. Anyway, he was going to be locked up for a very long time. I stopped thinking about him. He was out of my world now. He rode in the same police car as Matron. The cook went by ambulance because she had suffered smoke inhalation.

Matron looked back at me through the rear window. I couldn't see any life left in her eyes, not even sadness or defeat. There was nothing there, just two black coals. She had said that no grown-up would believe me, but it wasn't true.

Matron still seemed to believe her own lies even when the

police officers had surrounded her, like the samurai used to do when they surrounded the compound of a bad landlord.

"There he is!" she'd screamed pointing at me. "That boy started it all!"

They didn't believe her, of course.

Maybe she still didn't believe she was going to be put away for a century or more for what she'd done—and had tried to do.

The kids had won this one. I had explained some to the police when I called them earlier. "We're not losing this one," I'd said. "We're not gonna die," I'd said.

And the truth was all there to see in the light of the fire. It was the biggest in the world.

The moon is still casting its blue light over the castle. That's where I'm sitting right now. We're going to build it up again, stone by stone, tower by tower. It might not be possible right now, but one day we're going to do it. We've promised each other.

It smells of smoke from the camp. I'm not sure any of this can be explained. Things happen, sometimes because they have to, sometimes even though they don't have to. Sometimes it's horrible. And the most horrible things are the most difficult to explain.

I can hear sounds in the night. I'm alone now. I still have my *katana* and my *wakizashi* with me. The bird is still screeching out over the lake. It can't sleep either. It just flies around aimlessly and screeches. Soon the grebes will be up and so will the jackdaws and the gulls and the swans. Tomorrow, or today, I'm going to meet Kerstin. Maybe we'll just talk. I don't think she wants to practice *kenjutsu*—not right now, anyway. We're going to eat a good breakfast, too, now that the kitchen no longer exists. Grilled perch maybe. That's almost as good as the pieces of chocolate in the bag of Twist. They're finally where they belong. In my stomach. And in Sausage's and Kerstin's and Janne's, and everybody else's. The bag of Twist went a long way. No matter how many pieces I handed out, there were still plenty left in the bag.

Janne isn't here right now. He went into town with the explorers. The archer is going to ask his mom and dad if Janne can live with them instead of becoming a farmhand. My mother's supposed to be coming soon like all the other kids' parents or foster parents or whatever family they have. Mama's not on the run anymore. The police managed to find her somewhere way up in Norrland. I'll have to ask her what she was doing up there, if I have the energy. I don't have any energy left. But I'll be in touch sometime. From Japan maybe.